"You don't have to rattle off my attributes, Mr. Preston. I'm not someone who has to be praised to be happy." Ellie could sense he was smiling at her. Mocking her.

"Suit yourself." He settled into the seat. "I just didn't want you to feel threatened because I'm your boss, that's all."

He was gloating, pure and simple. "Why would that make me feel threatened?"

"I think you feel threatened because you don't like change."

She gasped. "Look, Cole, you know nothing about me, so please don't try to analyze me!"

She pulled onto the side of the road at the job site and jumped out of the car. Instead of taking the usual care when walking at a construction site, she plunged the heels of her shoes into the muddy ground. When she lifted her left leg, her shoe stayed put. She teetered and swayed like a bobble-headed, Hawaiian doll. Desperate to maintain her dignity, she jerked on her foot and fell into the waiting arms of Cole Preston.

## DIANN HUNT

and her husband, Jim, started on a three-mile trek through Amish country in 1997, and at that moment, she had no idea she was taking her first steps toward a new career. Inspired by their walk, she wrote an article, which was published a year later. Other articles soon followed. After studying fiction writing, she celebrated her first novella sale in 2001, with CBA bestselling novellas and novels reaching the bookshelves soon afterward.

Wanting to be used by God in the ministry of writing, Diann left her job as a court reporter in the fall of 2003 and now devotes her time to writing. Well, writing and spoiling her four granddaughters.

She has been happily married forever and loves her family, chocolate, her friends, chocolate, her dog and, well, chocolate.

Be sure to check out her Web site at www.diannhunt.com. Sign her guestbook, and drop her an e-mail. And, hey, if you have any chocolate…

# HEARTS UNDER CONSTRUCTION

## DIANN HUNT

Steeple
Hill®

Published by Steeple Hill Books™

STEEPLE HILL BOOKS

Steeple Hill®

ISBN 0-373-81220-5

HEARTS UNDER CONSTRUCTION

Copyright © 2005 by Diann Hunt

www.SteepleHill.com

Printed in U.S.A.

Therefore, if anyone is in Christ, he is a new creation; the old has gone, the new has come!

—*2 Corinthians* 5:17

To my editor, Krista Stroever, for her
encouragement and valuable expertise,
and to my critique partner, Colleen Coble,
for her prayers, writing advice and,
most of all, for her friendship.

In memory of my husband's grandparents,
James and Zana Hunt. I will never forget you.
Your Christian example lingers in my heart
still, and because of you, my life is changed.

# Chapter One

Change.

Some people liked it, even thrived on it. Eleanore Williams knew she wasn't one of them.

With a quick glance in her car mirror, Ellie smoothed her blond hair into place and touched up her makeup. She wiped away a smudge of mascara and felt pleased with the way her new emerald-green pantsuit matched her eyes.

When she stepped from her car into the morning light, the warmth of the sun's rays announced spring would soon slip into summer. It didn't seem possible. Where did the time go?

She tugged on the shoulder strap of her laptop, adjusting the weight of it as she walked toward the office. Oh, some changes were okay. Like getting a job promotion. She looked forward to that one. Change of clothes, change of soap detergent, change of seasons, she could handle those. It was the life upheavals she didn't like. The unexpected things. Okay, and diets. She hated diets. Yet, thanks to her father's side of the family, her five-foot-two frame swelled with every piece of chocolate almost from the instant it melted in her mouth. She thought of the apple and salad in her lunch bag. Her mood darkened. A large black ant crawled in her path and Ellie resisted the urge to crunch it into oblivion.

As a talented music minister, her father was always in high demand. With those calls had come many moves and upheavals. She supposed that was why she craved stability now. A slight breeze scented the air with lilac from a nearby bush. Now that was one thing on which she could always depend. The fragrance triumphed over her stomach, chasing away her gloomy mood. She smiled at the lilac bush, feeling thankful for the little things in life.

In spite of it being a Monday morning, she pushed through the doors of Wiley's Dream Homes with enthusiasm. The office already buzzed with activity. Jackson Wiley, owner of Wiley's Dream Homes, stood at the end of the room talking with a man whose back was to her. Ellie scooted into her seat and clicked on the computer. While waiting for it to start up, she picked through the stack of paperwork she had left on Friday.

A quick review told her before she could cope with the documents and a brand-new workweek, she would need a big cup of coffee. Snatching her favorite mug, which read "Hand over your chocolate and no one gets hurt," in large brown letters, she looked once more toward Jax before rising to make her way to the kitchen. This time both men were facing her. She decided the stranger beside Jax must be a new client. Then again, maybe not.

Feeling a bit curious, Ellie sat back down and eyed them further. As they stood together she could see the stark contrast between the two. Jax stretched to just about five foot eight in his thickest-heeled shoes. His brown hair was almost as long as Ellie's, stopping just under the earlobes. Small stylish glasses framed blue eyes, making him look every inch the professor. He looked uncomfortable in his suit and tie, like a snake wanting to shed its skin. Sweaters or relaxed shirts and work pants appealed to him.

Ellie guessed the man beside Jax at six feet. His long legs stretched nicely into casual jeans and a brown T-shirt spread tightly across his broad shoulders. A light gel held his dark, wavy hair perfectly in place. Stylish sideburns ended where his firm jaw began.

They laughed and Jax slapped the other man good-naturedly on the back. Interesting. Jax didn't usually chum around with clients or employee candidates like that. Her eyes narrowed. She concentrated hard, trying to figure out the identity of this stranger.

The men looked up in time to catch her indulging in the shameless scrutiny. Ellie felt her face burn. She swallowed a silent gulp and turned away, deciding now was a good time to visit the kitchen.

She glanced at her watch. In fifteen minutes, she would meet with Jax. She figured she had time to grab a quick cup of plain coffee with sugar—since there were no mochas available—and prepare for the good news. After all, she felt sure today he would offer her the partnership. This was one change for which she was ready. Jax had spent considerable time contemplating the matter of replacing his former partner who had retired in the early part of the year. On

Friday, he had told the sales staff he would announce the new partner on Monday. He had started to talk to her about the matter last week, but a telephone call had interrupted their conversation. Had he been going to offer it to her then? A shiver ran through her.

Ellie had worked hard to prove herself in the past couple of years. In her opinion, the other salespeople didn't seem to care as much about the company. It seemed logical for Jax to pick her for the position.

Arriving at the coffeemaker, she poured herself a cup of the hot liquid. She had always liked the smell of coffee better than the actual taste, but like the masses, she had learned to acquire a tolerable acceptance of the brew. From the counter, a cream-filled doughnut called to her, but she ignored it, deciding her nervous stomach couldn't handle it this morning.

Turning from the doughnut, she leaned her back against the counter and took a sip from her mug. Ellie mentally reviewed her wardrobe and thought of the new clothes she might purchase. Her things were growing threadbare, after all. A slight movement in the hallway caught her attention. The stranger was walking toward her.

She straightened herself, placed her mug on the counter, and turned to the man whose woodsy scent reached her before he did.

"Good morning." Tall and confident, he thrust his hand toward her. "I'm Cole Preston." She liked the way he said that. Confident and…soothing. Definitely soothing. Like raindrops pattering against a rooftop on a chilly afternoon.

She pulled out her best smile. "Ellie Williams." Eyes the color of coffee beans gazed down at her. His warm hand dwarfed her own. Something about him made her want to snuggle into a blanket by a roaring campfire and sing "Kumbayah."

He nodded with recognition. "I've heard a lot of good things about you."

His comment surprised her. She wondered why Jax would talk about her to this man. Still, strains of "Kumbayah" persisted. "Oh?"

"Um-hum. Jax says you're a great employee."

They stood silent a moment while Ellie tried to figure out where this whole conversation was going.

"Guess partners discuss such things." His teeth sparkled like a toothpaste advertisement.

She stared at him, wondering if she had heard right.

He kept smiling. "I've just signed on as Jax's new partner," he announced, practically rocking on his heels. "I guess I shouldn't have announced it until he does, but since you're his right-hand gal, as he puts it, I thought I could tell you."

"Kumbayah" came to a warbling halt. "P-p-p-partner?"

He shoved his hand into his pocket and nodded with an air of superiority. Before she could utter a word, Jax strolled up beside her. "Good, I see you've met Cole," he said with a nod and a grin. Jax looked at Ellie, then Cole, then back to Ellie. He raised his eyebrows, his smile faded. "Everything okay?"

"Everything's fine," she managed through clenched teeth.

Cole just stood there. Smiling. "I told her the news."

Jax gave a hesitant nod. "Oh."

Cole kept smiling.

Ellie wanted to cry, but Cole's gloating pushed her to anger, keeping her tears in check.

"Do we have a meeting, Ellie?" Jax asked, glancing at his watch.

"Yes," Ellie said with as bright a tone as she could muster.

"Could we scoot that back an hour? I have a few things to attend to."

"Sure, no problem." No hurry to get to the meeting now. Ellie reached deep within herself for some semblance of civility and turned to the new partner. "Well, Mr. Preston, welcome aboard."

"Please, call me Cole."

She wanted to call him something else all right, but Cole wasn't it. "Cole," she said with all the warmth of an iced mocha.

Ellie made a beeline for the bathroom. Her hands trembled and her chin started to quiver. She couldn't let anyone see her like this.

Once inside the empty bathroom, she locked herself in a stall, allowing silent tears to drop. How could Jax betray her? Why didn't he give her a chance? *Father, I thought this was all settled.* Her heart told her she had settled the matter. God had not. It took a few moments for her to swallow that revelation. Once again, she had jumped ahead of the Lord. Still, how could this not be the best thing for her? Hadn't she earned it?

What did her reading in I Samuel 15 say this morning? She strained to remember. Feeling puffed up with a victory in battle, King Saul decided he knew best and disobeyed the Word of the Lord.

Pride bred disobedience.

Like Saul, had Ellie taken matters into her own hands? She prayed a rote prayer for forgiveness, barely aware of the proud seed of bitterness that took root in a corner of her heart.

She yanked some toilet paper from the roll and dabbed at her face. Thankful that the room was empty, she stepped out of the stall and checked her makeup in the mirror. Tidying her hair, she looked at her reflection. "Well, it's time to buck up." She took a deep breath and walked through the door.

Morgan Somerville, another sales associate, approached. "Hey, Ellie, did you meet the new partner?"

Ellie nodded and kept walking as if she had an important meeting. Which, of course, she did not. Her meeting wasn't for another hour and the partnership news was already out.

Morgan whistled. "He can be *my* boss any day of the week."

Ellie looked at her with a forced smile, then turned and walked toward her desk. She groaned when she realized she had left her mug in the kitchen. Jax and Cole had been standing near the counter by her mug when she left. She decided to get her spare mug from the drawer so she wouldn't have to talk to them. Pulling out the bottom drawer of her desk, she reached in and lifted out a spare. Today, she decided, she needed her coffee more than ever. Mug in hand, she headed for the kitchen.

She couldn't understand why Jax hadn't considered her for the position. Perhaps he had, but why then had he chosen Cole? She tried to deny her wounded pride. This would not be a simple hurdle to overcome. The more she thought about the whole thing, the angrier she got. With her mind fixed firmly on the matter, she didn't notice someone else in the kitchen. Lost in thought, she all but plowed into the source of her distress and nearly bowled him over. Her coffee mug dropped from her hand, scattering into chunks of splintered fragments across the ceramic tile. As she teetered, Cole's hands clamped around her upper arms. "Are you all right?"

She wanted to plant her fists on her hips and say, "No, I'm not all right. If I were all right, my coffee mug would be in my hand, not shredded across the kitchen floor." Instead she said with more calm than she felt, "I'm fine." She brushed the flecks of white glass from her pantsuit. "I'm sorry. I don't know what I was thinking." Okay, maybe she did know what she had been thinking. Confident she had picked off the last speck, she glanced up. Cole smiled. That unnerved her. "I'll just get the broom and dustpan."

"Here, let me help you." He followed her toward a kitchen closet.

She hurried to the door ahead of him and said firmly, "Thank you, no." She had lost enough dignity for one day and didn't care to appear the helpless female.

"Oh, the independent type. Remember, we'll have to learn to work together."

Searching for, but not finding, a civil way to respond, she clamped her mouth shut.

"Excuse me, Mr. Preston. Jax would like to see you in his office." Alexandra Cassle, or Alex, as she preferred to be called, pasted on her most beautiful smile. Now there was a woman who never had to diet. Alex could eat a full plate of fettuccini smothered in Alfredo sauce every day of the week, and it would never affect her slender figure in the least.

Ellie struggled to keep her thoughts Christian.

Watching Cole look Alex over with appreciation, Ellie expected him to start foaming at the mouth at any moment, just like every other male who entered the office. She watched the scenario with interest, wondering if Jax knew he might have some competition. After all, Jax and Alex had been dating for, what, six months now? This little scenario could have real humor potential.

"Thank you. I've been there, but would you mind showing me where it is once more?"

Alex swung her thick chestnut waves behind her shoulders, batted her lashes a couple of times and let out a feminine chuckle.

Ellie stared in awe—at a true master at work.

"I'd be glad to, Mr. Preston. Just follow me."

"Please, call me Cole." His voice faded down the hall as he walked away without so much as a backward glance.

Yes, real potential, indeed.

Ellie mentally shook off the thought and shrugged. Maybe she was just jealous because she didn't know how to hook a man. Her thoughts stopped abruptly. What was she thinking? Hook a man like that! The very man who had stolen her job promotion? Her dreams? Her future?

She started to move and heard a crunch. Only then did she remember the puddle of broken crockery.

* * *

Cole settled into the cranberry leather chair across from Jax's desk. Alex walked out the door, closing it behind her.

Cole let out a low whistle and smiled at Jax.

"Careful, that's my woman, you know."

Cole raised his eyebrows and hid a smile behind a drink of coffee. "You two serious?"

Jax shrugged. "Alex is a nice girl. I'm not sure that it's serious, but I'm not ready for someone else to cut in."

Cole held up his hands. "You'll get no problem from me. I'll have my hands full just learning this business and trying to keep your best employee happy."

Jax laughed. "You mean Ellie?"

Cole whistled and rolled his eyes. "She's got her hackles up, that's for sure. Why didn't you warn me? It's obvious she wanted to be your partner."

Elbows on the desk, Jax dropped his chin into his hands. "I know. But she just wasn't ready for the responsibility." He thought a moment and leaned back in his chair, plopping his feet on his desk. "Now, don't get me wrong, Ellie works hard. But, well, I'm not sure she could handle all the aspects of the job." He looked away a moment. "I didn't mean to hurt her, though. She's not only my best employee, she's also a good friend. I should have warned her." He turned back to Cole. "Then she wouldn't have taken it out on you."

"Yeah, thanks a lot."

"I think you can handle yourself." Jax smiled. "As I told you, I'm taking some classes with an eye to teaching at the local college eventually. Right now, I need the business to help fund my education, but one day I'm hoping to be able to sell it, when I've completed the education requirements and when the right buyer comes along.

"That means I need someone like you for the position, with more experience and a more forceful personality. Ellie's too nice to deal with some of those tough guys on the home sites. And I just don't think she could handle it alone."

Cole piped up. "Remember, this is a trial thing. I'm not sure I'm ready for a lifetime commitment. We're just trying this thing out, right?"

"I know all about you and commitments. That's why you're not married." Jax laughed.

"And *your* excuse is?"

Jax shrugged. "Seriously, Cole, I appreciate you at least giving this job arrangement a chance. The business needs someone like you. We both know your reputation. You're not afraid to let someone go, if need be. You've got a good business head on your shoulders." Jax twirled a pencil between his fingers. "Lucky for me, the advertising company in Chicago had a corporate takeover. When you told me you'd lost your job, this seemed the perfect fit. For both of us. Of course, I know you'll miss the adventure, the travels, the million-dollar clients."

Cole shrugged. "Those things have their place. But they come with headaches, too. I'm ready for a change."

Jax lowered his feet to the floor, laid the pencil on his desk, and picked up his coffee. "I'm glad to hear that. I was hoping you could manage to stick around long enough to make some money here." Jax winked before sipping his drink.

Cole shrugged. "Okay, so I'm not exactly Stanley Stability. You don't have to go into my sordid past. I'm turning over a new leaf. Otherwise, I wouldn't have accepted."

Jax cocked an eyebrow. "So, why the sudden change of heart?"

Cole looked toward the window. "I'm not sure. Just feels like this is right, you know?"

"Good. I knew I was taking a risk when I asked you. I'd hoped you would stay." Jax quickly added, "But I understand it's a trial thing. No promises."

Cole nodded.

A knock on the door caused them to turn.

"Come in," Jax said.

Ellie stepped inside and paused. "Oh, sorry, I didn't know you had someone still with you."

Jax perked up. "No, no, come on in, Ellie." He stood and walked over to her.

"I need to be going, anyway," Cole said.

Jax closed the door then turned to them. "No, I need to talk to both of you, won't you sit down?"

Cole settled back into his chair, and Ellie sat down in the remaining one beside him. Jax returned to his seat. "We're going to be working closely together. All of us." Jax looked at them in turn. "Cole's going to relieve me of some of my responsibilities out on the job sites."

"But, I—"

Jax held up his hand. "I know you've been doing that, Ellie, but it's too much for one person. Of course—"

"Too much for one person, Jax? Have I not handled things well by myself? Remember the Ollis job? Didn't I come through for you when there was a mix-up with the contractors? How about the Person house, didn't I handle the cabinetry problem without your help?"

"Well, yes, Ellie, you did, but—"

"Then I don't see why we need to change things. We were handling situations just fine before. Why the change? Why couldn't you leave things as they were? It makes no sense, Jax." Her eyes flashed, she straightened in her chair. "Just last week, wasn't I the one who wouldn't give up when—"

Jax held up his hand to silence her, but anger wouldn't shake her free.

"—the Mills were—"

"Ellie."

"—angry about the—"

"Ellie."

"—foundation crack? Didn't I put in extra hours to get that matter settled? And when—"

"Ellie, enough." Jax's eyes pinned her. "As I was saying, Cole will oversee things, and he'll need you to carry out assignments that he can't do."

She paused a moment, took a deep breath, then blew it out. "I see. In other words, he's my supervisor."

Jax studied the pencil in his hand before looking up at her. "Yes, Ellie, he is your supervisor."

Cole watched her. He knew she was upset, but he didn't know how to fix things. "Look, I—" He almost reached for her hand, but the look on her face stopped him cold.

Their eyes locked for one electric moment. "That's fine. I'm glad I don't have to do all of that by myself anymore. Makes my job easier."

Jax put on a pleasant expression. "Great."

Alex rang over the intercom, notifying Jax of an important call. The three decided to meet later.

Cole followed Ellie out the door, not nearly as convinced as Jax that things would be so great.

# Chapter Two

The next morning, after making the necessary notations, Ellie shook hands with the Wilsons and said goodbye. She felt energized after every house deal. Of course, things didn't always run smoothly, and the pesky modifications could drive her crazy at times, but all in all, she decided, she loved her job. Maybe she'd reward herself with a mocha.

She heard Jax's voice as she neared his office. Perhaps now was not a good time. But Jax had insisted that since they hadn't met again yesterday, due to unexpected calls, he wanted to meet with her today. She peeked around the doorway. Still talking on the phone, he motioned her to enter. Ellie took her place in the chair.

"All right, Chad, do what you need to do

to keep them happy. Drop the price, throw in the appliances, whatever."

Jax lifted a weak smile toward Ellie and shrugged.

Poor Jax. Business was not his forte. He wanted to teach. Who could have known his father and mother would die in an auto accident and leave him the family company? It saddled him with a profession he wouldn't have chosen for himself.

Jax hung up the phone. He smiled and leaned over the desk. "So what can I do for one of my favorite employees?"

"You'd better be careful. Alex might hear you," she teased.

He waved off the matter and reached for his mug of coffee. "We're not exactly engaged, you know."

Ellie smiled at her friend; Jax was more like a brother than a boss. They'd met six years prior when his family had joined her church.

After a quick swallow, Jax put his cup down and looked at her. "I guess you want to know about Cole?"

"Well, the thought had crossed my mind." She smiled at him. "You don't owe me an explanation, Jax, but—"

He held up his hand to stop her. "It's all right. You have a right to know what's going on."

Jax got up and walked over to close the door. He settled back into his chair and took a deep breath. His eyes fixed on his desk. "It's like this, Ellie." He stopped long enough to look up at her. "I needed someone to relieve me of some responsibilities."

"But why—why Cole?"

Jax gave her a sympathetic look. He got up and walked around the desk to the chair across from her. "Look, Ellie." He grabbed her hand. "You're an excellent worker. I know you wanted this promotion, and I'm sorry I couldn't offer it to you, but honestly, Cole has more experience in the business realm. He's just a better fit for the job."

"So you feel he is more qualified?" Her nose pointed up.

Jax nodded. "It's not that he's better than you, just more experienced."

The words pierced her pride, exposing raw layers of pain. She said nothing.

"Things won't change all that much. You'll go on doing what you've been doing."

"But you said yourself he is my supervisor, right?" She knew her question sounded childish, but right now she didn't care.

Jax shrugged. "I guess, technically, yes. But you don't have anything to worry about." He squeezed her hand like an encouraging brother. "Your work is better than good enough. You're the main one keeping us going right now. If you weren't writing those offers and overseeing the construction sites, I don't know what I'd do. Chad, Morgan and Tim do their best, but they just don't have the drive that you do."

She softened. "I'm sorry, Jax. I'm just a little edgy."

"Dieting again?"

She winced a little before nodding.

"Ellie, you are perfect the way you are. Why do you always diet?"

"In case you haven't noticed, I like food. Fat grams stick to my body like leeches on reverse." Then in the moment of silence that stretched between them, she was struck with inspiration. "Want to go to lunch?"

"It's nine-thirty," he answered dryly.

He could be such a spoilsport.

Jax shook his head and walked back over to his seat behind the desk.

"So, what exactly is Cole going to be doing?"

"He'll be helping me some with the banks and financial side of things, but mostly, he'll be checking out job sites, gathering information, overseeing things."

"Like employees?"

Jax nodded and shrugged.

A knock sounded at the door. "Come in."

"Hey, two of my favorite people." Cole's smile almost chased away Ellie's bitterness.

Almost.

"May I come in?"

"Yes, I was just leaving, anyway." She stood and crossed the room. He stepped in front of her.

"Seems we're both always coming or going. Don't leave on my account." His eyes held her in place. Her breath caught in her throat. "Please." He said the last word for her ears only.

His scent, the depth in his voice, the intensity in his eyes, unnerved her. "I have to go," she squeaked. Quickly, she brushed past him and darted through the door. Once outside Jax's office, she gasped for air, realizing only then she had barely breathed from the moment their eyes met.

\* \* \*

After lunch Ellie gathered her things and walked toward the kitchen where she heard Jax's voice.

"I'll be back later, Jax. I'm headed to the Gregory job site," she told him.

Cole rounded the corner. "Hey, is it okay if I tag along? I need to check on some things."

Ellie stopped. "Well, uh—"

He held up his hand. "I won't bite, I promise."

Ellie wished she could make the same promise. Her lunch salad had done little to improve her spirits.

Cole looked at Jax. "I'll check on the mechanicals and make sure we've got the appropriate permits. Check on the guys' progress."

Ellie felt her face flame with heat. Those were her responsibilities. She glanced at Jax, but he quickly turned away. "I'll see you later." He waved them off and headed back toward his office.

Her mouth opened like a baby bird's at mealtime. She glanced up to see Cole staring at her and clamped her mouth closed.

Cole and Ellie walked outside to her car and climbed inside.

"Nice car," he said, stroking the leather upholstery.

"Thanks." Once she closed her door and started the engine, Ellie clicked on the radio station, turning it up loud enough to discourage any conversation. She knew this whole mess wasn't really Cole's fault, but who else could she blame? Jax was her friend and trying to run a business, she couldn't blame him. Things were what they were. She'd have to get used to it. Still, it would take a while for her wounded pride to heal.

Cole reached over and turned the volume down. "Do you mind if I talk to you for a minute?"

Great. Just what she wanted. "Sure, what's up?" She tried to make her words sound cheerful, as if his presence didn't bother her in the least. And it didn't, really. Though his cologne was a little distracting. Made her think of a log cabin in the woods. And, of course, a log cabin made her think of maple syrup and pancakes.

"Look, I don't know what happened, really, but for some reason, we got off to a bad start. I'd like to change that."

"There's no problem," she said, as if voicing it made it so.

"Come on, Ellie, we both know there's a problem. I know I can't fix it, but I'd like to start again."

"You can't fix it because there's nothing to fix." Couldn't he just let her lick her wounds and allow her time to get over the disappointment?

"He says you're a great worker—"

Oh, now he was patronizing her. "You don't have to rattle off my attributes, Mr. Preston. I'm not someone who has to be praised to be happy." Her breath came in short gasps, but she continued. "I'm not mad. There is no problem." She kept her gaze fixed on the road, her voice even and calm. Though she didn't look at him, she could sense he was smiling at her. A taunting smile. Mocking her. Okay, she might have to hurt him.

"Suit yourself." He settled into his seat. "I just didn't want you to feel threatened, that's all."

"Why would I feel threatened?" Now, he was making her really mad.

"Because I'm your boss."

He was gloating, pure and simple. "Why would that make me feel threatened?"

He shrugged. "I think you feel threatened because you don't like change."

She gasped and turned to him. "Look, Cole, you know nothing about me, so please don't try to analyze me!"

She pulled onto the side of the road at the job site, slammed into park with more force than she'd intended, and jumped out of the car. Cole followed suit. She knew she would regret her anger later, but for now it simmered like a sauna bath.

Instead of taking the usual care when walking at a construction site, she plunged the heels of her shoes into the muddy ground. When she lifted her left leg, her shoe stayed put. She teetered and swayed like a Hawaiian dashboard doll. Desperate to maintain her dignity, she jerked on her foot and fell into the waiting arms of Cole Preston.

The construction workers whistled and cawed from the house. Ellie wanted to curl up and roll away.

Cole whispered into her ear, "What shall we do for an encore?"

She turned a disgusted face at him and yanked herself free from his arms. "You are the most egotistical man I have ever met!"

He laughed out loud and bowed as she made her way past him.

Her only solace came from flicking specks of dirt from her shoes across his pant legs as she went.

Ellie took a sip from her teacup. "Thanks, Mom. This hits the spot."

"Your headache is better, then?"

Her mother's worried gaze met Ellie's. "I'm much better." Ellie could see her mom visibly relax. "What would I do without you?"

Her mom waved her hand. "You'd be just fine. The Lord would give you someone in my place."

"No one could ever take your place, Mom."

Her mother fidgeted with her teacup and glanced around the room. "Ellie, don't you think your couch would be more functional if you placed it against that wall? Then you could see out the patio while—"

"Oh, here we go. I've told you, Mom, I've got enough battle scars from my childhood. Remember? From when I bumped into furniture that you kept switching around the room?"

Her mother's mouth formed into a pout and she hung her head.

Ellie laughed, causing her mother to brighten.

"Don't you get bored with it the same way all the time?"

Ellie shook her head. "I like to keep things the way they are. Why fix something that's not broken?"

Her mother remained silent, giving in on the issue as if it were the first time, though they had had the discussion many times before. "Ellie, your headaches usually come on because of stress. Anything you want to talk about?"

Ellie put her cup on the coffee table, straightened her pillow and leaned against the back of the sofa. "It's Cole Preston. I try, Mom, I really do, but I just don't like the man."

"What is it you don't like about him?"

"Everything. He's pushy. He's demanding. Always trying something new."

"Ah."

"Ah, what?" Ellie couldn't hide the edginess in her voice.

"Well, honey, it's just that you've never adjusted well to change."

"Mom, please, I'm not a child anymore. I can adapt."

Her mother raised an eyebrow.

"I can," she repeated, defensively. They sat a moment in silence. She hated it when her mother was right. "Okay, so I don't like change," she admitted with some reluctance. Ellie sighed and adjusted her blankets. She looked at her mother. "I'm still struggling with this whole partnership thing."

"Really?"

"Well, it's just not fair." Oh, she could kick herself for sounding so childish. Her mother stared, saying nothing. Ellie felt like a bug under a microscope. With everything in her, she tried not to squirm. She knew she was wrong. She had to let her bitterness go, but could she? Sighing, she leaned back into her pillow.

"I wouldn't worry too much about it, Ellie. As you get used to his ways, you'll get along fine." Her mother smiled.

Ever the optimist, Ellie thought. "Is Dad coming for dinner?"

Her mother came over and fluffed the blanket around her. "Yes. In another hour or so."

"The vegetable soup smells so good."

"You'd get a decent meal once in a while if you could get away from work long enough to come to our house. I had an awful time finding enough food in your cupboards to come up with dinner." Her mother finished the last tuck on the blanket and stood up. "By the way, why do you have so much cabbage in your refrigerator?"

Thoughts of the new soup diet came to her. She'd only been on it for two days and already the thought of cabbage made her want to pulverize the pale green heads when she passed them in the produce section of her grocery store. She never told her mother when she went on diets. Her mother always complained about today's women being too thin. According to her mother, unless a woman carried an extra twenty pounds, she looked sickly.

Ellie loved her mother.

"I heard cabbage is good for you."

Her mother eyed Ellie warily. Nothing gets past Mom. Ellie closed her eyes in hopes of stopping further discussion about the cabbage.

"Sounds like you've got a few things to pray about." Her mother rubbed a warm cloth against Ellie's forehead.

Ellie smiled. Her mother's answer to everything: "Pray about it." Ellie knew she was right, but something stopped her when she tried to pray about Cole. She dismissed the thought that her attitude was wrong when she approached the matter with the Lord.

Her mother said something else, but the words were lost in a hazy dreamworld. A world of stability where things didn't change, where she felt safe.

A world without Cole Preston.

## Chapter Three

The next week passed in a blur. Chaos in the office kept Jax and Cole busy. Ellie worked hard to avoid them both. She was tired by the time Friday arrived, and felt relieved when five o'clock rolled around. With a glance at the clock, she grabbed her purse and walked from the office toward her car. The afternoon's winds had swept the sky clean as evening settled upon the city. Ellie pulled in a deep breath. The air smelled sweet with summer. Though she felt tired from a full day's work, stepping outside had revived her spirits.

Jax walked up beside her. "So, will you go with us tomorrow?"

She frowned.

"Come on, Ellie. It will be fun." He lifted

puppy-dog eyes to her, which always made her give in.

"Isn't it enough that I have to work with him every day, Jax? Must I see him on the weekends, too?"

"It's not like we do this every weekend. A trip to Chicago, a day of sailing on Lake Michigan. Please? I could use some relaxation, and Alex wants to go with another couple."

"Look, Jax, Lucy and Ricky Ricardo, they are a couple. Tom Hanks and Rita Wilson, they are a couple. Cole Preston and I work together. We are not a *couple*."

He stepped back and held up his hands. "I know, I know. I didn't mean you were a couple."

Ellie took a deep breath. "I hate like everything to do this, but I will do it for you, Jax. That is the only reason."

He smiled like a dieter who'd lost another pound—a smile she hadn't worn in weeks. He grabbed her with both hands and promptly placed a kiss on her forehead. "You're the best, Ellie."

She shook her head and smiled in spite of herself. "Just you remember this the next time you need a partner."

He groaned.

"Seriously, Jax, I'm doing this for you. The last thing I want to do on a Saturday is spend my day off with Cole Preston."

"Why don't you like him?"

She wasn't sure how to respond. After all, Cole was Jax's best friend. "Besides the fact he's got an ego the size of Texas?"

Jax threw back his head and laughed. "I guess he does at that. But then I need someone with confidence in the business."

Climbing into the car, she rolled down her window and looked up at him.

"We'll pick you up at seven o'clock tomorrow morning," he said.

With a reluctant nod, Ellie turned on the engine and pulled her car into gear. She waved goodbye and looked in her rearview mirror in time to see Cole join Jax in the parking lot. Her stomach knotted. With a glance at the glove compartment, she decided even the hidden candy bar could do little to calm her spirits. Just one day, she told herself. No big deal, right? She would go along for Jax's sake.

She took a deep breath; the tomato-juice diet wasn't working and it made her too edgy. Someone at the office had told her about a new low-carb diet. She decided she'd like to try that one. Once her car pulled up at the traffic light, Ellie glanced again at the glove compartment. Her fingers danced lightly on the steering wheel. The light stayed red. Finally, she reached over and pulled out the candy bar. Maybe she'd try the low-carb thing next week.

The doorbell rang much too soon. Ellie grabbed her canvas bag and purse then headed for the door.

"Good morning." Jax and Alex met her with a smile. She wondered why they both came to the door. *Probably afraid I would back out and it would take two of them to haul me, kicking and screaming, to the car.* She smiled with the thought.

"Hi." Although Ellie did not want to go on this outing, she had to admit she felt a twinge of excitement. The day already boasted of warmth, sunshine and fun. She followed Jax and Alex to the car, taking note of their appearance. Ellie decided Jax looked nice in his navy shorts, a white pullover with a navy collar and stylish sandals.

Auburn hair fanned across Alex's shoulders in waves. That color was reflected by a chunky necklace of browns and tans nestled at the throat of her cream-colored blouse. Brown shorts with a matching belt and sandals completed her outfit. At her side, she carried a cream wide-brimmed hat. She appeared to have just stepped out of a modeling shoot.

Ellie glanced down at her own sensible shorts outfit. They say you can tell a lot about people by the clothes they wear. She imagined her clothes said she hadn't glanced at a fashion magazine in months. Besides, the inside of a person was what really counted. She tried to ignore the storm gathering around her heart. Come to think of it, she wasn't exactly model material in that department, either.

"Beautiful day," she said, pulling on her seat belt.

"We're going to have so much fun!" Alex said with more enthusiasm than Ellie had ever seen from Jax's date. Ellie had to admit she was glad she had come after all.

Jax put on his sunglasses then edged the car out of the driveway.

"Did Cole already make arrangements to rent the boat, or will we have to do that when we get there?" Ellie asked.

"Oh, it's all taken care of. Seems he has a friend there who is loaning us his sailboat."

"Of course, he would think of everything," she muttered under her breath. She looked around the car then up at Jax through the mirror. "Did you bring any chocolate?"

Jax shook his head. "Eat your energy bar." He pulled into the blur of traffic.

Finally, at Cole's house, Jax went up to the door to let Cole know they were there. Alex chattered about what fun they were going to have, but Ellie didn't hear much once she saw Cole step outside. She watched as he lifted a cooler, placed it on the porch, then closed the door behind him. He caught up with Jax and walked toward the car. His long legs sported khaki shorts and he wore a comfortable shirt, revealing the strong arms of a disciplined man.

After some small talk, Jax turned on the radio and they settled into a comfortable ride. Ellie took a deep breath and decided now was as good a time as any to get things straightened out with Cole. She whispered so the others couldn't hear. "Hey, about the other day—"

"Forget it. I stepped out of bounds and I'm sorry."

The apology surprised her. "Me, too."

Cole smiled and winked, chasing the dark mood from her heart. She thought the day might turn out all right after all.

Once settled on the boat, a warm breeze carried them a good ways onto the lake. Ellie sat with her eyes closed, willing herself to relax in the comfort of the summer sun. Though the temperature rose to an uncomfortable degree on land, the wind lifted mists of lake water around them, making the air perfect.

Hearing Alex laugh, Ellie peeked over and saw Alex playfully jabbing Jax. Ellie turned away, not wanting to intrude upon their private moment, and glanced at Cole. His head was back, his face tilted heavenward. Golden sunlight sprayed across his already bronze body, causing his skin to glisten.

Confusion plagued her. She closed her eyes. Cole drove her crazy at work. Always changing things, putting new policies into place, new rules, new guidelines. Sometimes she thought he did it because he knew she hated change. Why would he want to make her life miserable? Was she miserable? Yes, though she wasn't sure why. Maybe she needed a new job. She loved working for Jax, but she knew he wanted to go into teaching someday. Why couldn't things stay the same? Why couldn't Jax be happy in the business? Then they wouldn't have this mess with Cole. Why couldn't people be content? Changes, changes and more changes. Nothing stayed the same.

*Lord, help me to stop looking at things through negative eyes. I'm sure my attitude has been less than pleasing to You, and I'm sorry. Whatever You want for my future, Father, help me to leave that in Your hands.*

"You still with us?"

Ellie opened her eyes to see Cole. Her heart jumped like a playful fish on the water's surface. "Uh-huh."

He opened a can of pop. "It's a great day for this."

"It's absolutely wonderful." She closed her eyes again.

"You hungry?" Cole asked. Ellie straightened, attempting to shake off the lethargy. He obviously didn't know her well.

"Trust me, she's hungry," Jax piped up before she had a chance to answer. They all laughed.

Alex and Ellie pulled the sandwiches and soft drinks from the cooler while the guys checked the boat's course.

"Are you having a good time?"

Ellie thought for a moment. "Yeah, I really am."

Alex chuckled. "You said that as if you're surprised."

Ellie smiled. "I guess I did."

"And are you?"

"What?"

"Surprised that you're having a good time."

Ellie shrugged.

"You work too hard, Ellie. What fun is that?" Alex pulled the tab on her pop and took a drink.

Ellie watched her but said nothing.

Alex wiped her mouth. "You know what they say, 'All work, no play makes Ellie a dull girl.'"

Ellie knew there was truth in what Alex said. Not only that, but Ellie's hard work hadn't exactly paid off. She pushed the thought away, not allowing it to spoil her day. "You and Jax seem to be having a good time."

Alex lifted a haughty smile. "And why not? We're practically engaged."

"Oh?"

"Well, not officially, but I'm sure he'll pop the question soon."

Ellie knew Jax pretty well and didn't think he was quite ready for that step. In her own spoiled way, Alex seemed to contribute more to the relationship than Jax.

The rest of the day passed as quickly as the gentle breeze. Weary, but happily so, they finally settled into the car as Jax headed the car toward home.

"It's been a great day, Jax. Thanks for driving," Cole said from the backseat. Everyone agreed.

Cole looked at Ellie. "I had a great time with you, too." Before she could linger in the sudden warmth that sprang up at his words, he added, "Oh, by the way, we need to go over the list of contractors next week. Deleting a few, adding some others."

The impact of his words hit her with full force. "Deleting?"

"Yeah, I'm letting some go."

"Why?" She knew the answer before she asked. There were a couple of men who always showed up late. But did Cole realize these men had legitimate excuses? One had to drop off his children at the daycare, another had to wait until his wife got home from work to pass off their only car. He came in usually twenty minutes late. She could live with that. After all, he didn't get paid for the time he wasn't there. Didn't Cole have any compassion at all?

"Let me just say I have my reasons."

Oh, fine, he didn't feel he owed her an explanation. He was, after all, her supervisor. Who was she kidding? Coleman Preston infuriated her. If she'd been a dragon, she'd have turned him to toast. "I'm sure you do." She scooted herself farther away from him and closer to the door, turning her gaze out the window.

The man was insufferable.

Cole had been out of the office most of the day on Monday. Ellie assumed he was dealing with the contractors. She had to let it go.

On Tuesday morning, she sat at her desk and pulled open the first file needing her attention.

"Ellie, do you have a minute?"

Swiveling her chair around, she saw Cole standing in front of her. "Yes."

He pulled up a chair. "I just wanted to let you know the Wilsons called last night. Mrs. Wilson wanted to check on a couple of wall measurements for furniture placement or something. Anyway, you were gone and the matter seemed urgent to them, so I met them at the house last night."

Ellie felt her defenses going up. She tried to stay calm. After all, he'd done her a favor. She should be grateful.

"Thank you," she managed to say with some effort.

"They're nice people. Had a good visit with them. We started talking about carpeting, and well, I laid carpet when I was in high school and told them a little about what I know. They asked me if I could help them pick the carpet for their home."

Is there anything he hasn't done? Anger scorched the pit of her stomach. "Cole, I'm supposed to help them do that."

"Yeah, I know, that's why I'm telling you. I figured you wouldn't care since we all want what's best for the customer, right?"

"Are you what's best for the customer?" She kept her voice low and controlled, though inside her emotions ran rampant. He had gone too far. He might be her boss, but they were *her* customers. She knew she didn't trust him for a reason.

"Look, I know a little about carpeting, that's all. What's your problem, anyway?"

She took a deep breath and rubbed her

forehead. There had to be another way of dealing with this besides acting like a crazy woman. She needed to prove herself. Show Jax he had made a mistake in hiring Cole. She thought she had already proven herself; what more could she do?

"Ellie?"

She looked at him.

"I thought we had settled this whole thing between us. What's the deal?"

"The deal is I would appreciate you letting me handle my own clients, Cole. I don't think that's too much to ask."

"You know I didn't mean to get in the way, it just sort of happened."

Yeah, like you getting in the way of my partnership offer, she wanted to say, but for once, she held her tongue. She glanced at her watch. "I have to go."

His eyebrows lifted.

"If it's all right with you, I have an appointment to talk to a couple about building a house." She lifted her chin, refusing to blink her eyes.

He bowed, stepped aside and made a grand sweeping gesture with his hand.

They would discuss the matter again.

He could be sure of that.

* * *

That evening, Ellie sat on the couch in the living room at her parents' home. She tried to look through a magazine, but felt too restless to enjoy it. Giving up, she plunked it back on the coffee table.

Ellie looked up to see her dad watching her.

"Want to talk about it?"

"Dad, I can't help it. Cole makes me so mad I can't think straight."

"Come on, Sunshine, you really think he's trying to steal your clients?"

She didn't want him to call her by that name just now. It didn't fit. "Well, I told you what he did. What do you think?"

"Could it be he really was just trying to help?"

"Oh, I don't know what to think anymore. I feel like I'm the only one who can see through him."

"Is that how it is?"

"What do you mean?"

"You're the only one who can see this matter clearly?"

She realized how ridiculous she sounded. A long exhale escaped her.

Her mom entered the room with a tray of

drinks. "I understand how she's feeling, really."

Ellie grabbed her drink from the tray. "Thanks, Mom."

"No, I mean it." She offered Ellie's dad his drink and settled into her seat with her own. "He did seem to overstep his bounds with her clients."

Her dad took a drink of his pop. "Men don't think that way. I see it as him trying to help. You know we've tried to teach you to look for the best in people. Have you done that with Cole?"

Her dad always knew how to go straight to the source of the problem and pluck the truth right out. His eyes searched hers. She kept silent.

"Something to think about."

"What am I supposed to do, let him take over my clients while I sit and do nothing?"

"Why not go along?" With a straw, her mother stirred her ice cubes, causing them to rattle against the glass.

"Great idea, Debbie."

"What's a great idea? I don't get it."

"Go with Cole when he meets with the Wilsons to talk about their carpet. That way, you're both represented, the clients get what they want, and your position stays intact. He gets what he wants by pleasing the clients, if indeed that truly is his motive."

Ever so slightly, Ellie brightened with the idea. "I'll do just that." She stared into the distance and rubbed her chin. "He won't be able to take over, and I'll be there to monitor his activities and conversation."

"Right," her dad added. Her parents relaxed into their chairs, seeming pleased with the discussion.

Ellie looked at them and smiled. She would call the Wilsons when she got home to schedule a meeting, then she would inform Cole at the office in the morning. If he couldn't meet them, so be it. If he could, fine. She'd be there, too. She drank her pop and allowed herself to relax a little. Maybe it would work.

Cole Preston might try to get the better of her, but she was not about to make it easy for him.

## Chapter Four

The next morning Ellie felt almost exhilarated with the challenge of facing Cole. She'd stand her ground and he would no doubt back out, not wanting her to go to Jax. He might be able to schmooze his way with other people, but she would not be so easily fooled. Besides, he was there to help Jax with the business, not gather his own list of clients.

She walked into the office with confidence and marched right over to Cole who was standing by Alex's desk, chatting with her. "I need to talk to you, Cole, when you have a minute."

Ellie watched as he shot Alex an oh-brother-here-we-go look. Her resolve started to melt. She caught herself. No, she couldn't give in now. She was almost there.

They walked over to Ellie's desk. She tried to ignore the curious stares coming their way. Dropping her purse down on her desk, she pulled a chair up for him, sat down, and waited for him to sit. "I called the Wilsons last night, and we are to meet them at Fine Floors at six-thirty tonight to talk over their selection together."

Cole gave her a grin as if he knew exactly what she was doing. "Great. I'll be there."

His comment took her by surprise. She had at least expected some sort of confrontation.

"Do you want to work overtime and just leave together from here?" he asked.

She had to think quickly. The last thing she wanted to do was ride with him. "Um, no, I need to go home first."

"Okay, rather than have two cars, I'll swing by and pick you up at your house around six o'clock," Cole said.

Great. This was not going at all the way she had planned. "You don't know where I live."

"Yeah, I do."

How did he know that? Why did he know that? "But—"

"I'll see you then, Ellie." Cole got up and walked away.

No matter how hard she tried, she could not figure him out one bit and it made her crazy. Well, she'd be on her guard. Regardless of what anyone else said, she didn't trust him.

Ellie spent the day in a flurry of work, for which she was grateful. It gave her less time to worry about Cole and his latest antics.

She walked up to Jax in the kitchen. "I'm leaving now, is that all right?"

He glanced at the clock above the sink. "So soon?"

She followed his gaze. "I know it's fifteen minutes early, but remember, I told you Cole is picking me up at six o'clock to meet the Wilsons. I was hoping to have a little time to freshen up before we go."

"Oh, right. I forgot." He opened the refrigerator. "Do you know who brought in all this grapefruit?"

She bit her lip.

"Another diet?"

She shrugged.

He shook his head and grabbed a chocolate bar tucked in the back of the top shelf. "Whose are these?"

Ellie hated being caught. She looked

around the room as if she hadn't a clue what he was talking about.

"Ellie?" He peered at her over the rim of his glasses.

She could almost feel herself seated in the middle of a dark, empty room with a bright incandescent bulb hanging over her. She imagined sweat forming over her brow. The pressure caused her to crack. "Okay, fine. They're mine."

He shook his head and began to unwrap the bar.

She ignored him. "So, is it okay if I leave? I'm not going to have time to eat dinner before then the way it is."

"No dinner? Be kind to the customers."

"Ha, ha," she said with exaggerated sarcasm.

"You want one of these?" He extended the candy bar toward her.

"No, thanks. I'm on a diet."

Jax shook his head. "You're pathetic."

She smiled at his teasing. "I know."

"Ellie?" He grew serious a moment. "You be careful. I mean, Cole's my best friend and all, but he's broken a few hearts."

"Don't you even talk like that. I can barely stay in the same room with the man, let alone feel any attraction to him."

Jax shrugged. "Okay, just wanted to make sure. I've seen him change the mind of more than one woman."

"I'm not easily changed, remember?"

By the time Ellie heard Cole's car pull up to her house, she had just completed the finishing touches on her makeup. She took one last glance at herself in the mirror. After changing from the blue dress she had worn to the office, she'd put on her black pantsuit. Though professional, it appeared more casual than the dress and much more appropriate for visiting a carpet store. She fluffed the back of her hair and grabbed her purse.

Thinking Cole was waiting in his car, Ellie started to bolt out of the door only to bump into him standing in the doorway. "Oh, I'm sorry." Their noses were inches apart. He held her arms to steady her.

"We seem to do this a lot." His eyes teased her.

Very uncomfortable with the feeling that shot through her, she pulled away. "I thought you were in your car."

"Dost thou think me not a gentleman, fair lady?"

She couldn't help but smile.

"How could I not escort one so attractive?"

Uh-oh, Jax was right. This man was spinning his web. No doubt to get her to share her commission. She ignored his comment. She fairly shoved him out of the way so she could lock the front door. When she turned around, she found him still standing close beside her. She straightened, and in businesslike fashion, walked to his navy SUV. He followed close behind and opened the door for her.

He made her feel like a teenager going on her first date. The sooner she got this appointment over, the better. Oh, why had she agreed to ride with him?

They made their way down the road, talking of surface matters. She tried not to look at him. She told herself it had nothing to do with being afraid of getting caught by his spell.

The appointment passed quickly. The Wilsons were happy with their final choices. Ellie had to admit Cole did know a lot about choosing carpet. She was also surprised he had let her control the meeting and even brought her into the conversation when he shared his knowledge of the carpet they'd picked. All in all, things went much better than she had expected. They said their goodbyes and got back in Cole's car.

He turned on the ignition then looked at her. "I don't know about you, but I'm famished. Want to stop and get something to eat?"

As if right on cue, her stomach growled. She clutched it with her hand.

"I'll take that as a yes?"

They both laughed. She didn't want to eat with him, but she had to admit she was hungry. A meal wouldn't be too excruciating.

Once they were seated in a booth at the steak house, the waitress approached them. Ellie wanted ice water with lemon. Cole ordered a soft drink.

They sat in silence while looking over the menus. A country-and-western singer crooned over the speaker. Soft conversation rippled around them, and the smell of frying steak wafted through the room. Once they'd made their meal choices, Cole and Ellie stacked their menus on the table so the waitress could collect them.

"What are you getting?"

"I'm blowing my diet for tonight. I'm ordering steak in a southwestern sauce and chunky fries."

"Trust me, those fries aren't going to hurt you. You look great." His smile jolted

through her. What in the world was going on
with her?

"Let's keep this strictly on a professional
level, okay?" There, she'd put him in his
place.

"You think I want anything more than
that?" His words sounded as though the very
idea couldn't be farther from his mind.

"Well, I—" Oh dear, she was growing pink
again. She could feel it. Once again, she had
presumed too much. Of course he wasn't interested in her in that way. She rooted through
her purse to cover her embarrassment.

"I'm sure you already have a special someone?" His eyebrows lifted queryingly as if he
knew she couldn't possibly have anyone in
her life.

Oh, he lit her fire like a match to a torch.
She lifted her chin and said with utmost dignity, "I belong to no one. Except God." She
almost felt embarrassed to add God to the
mix, feeling quite sure she hadn't represented
Him well at all in front of Cole.

His eyes widened. "Oh, my mistake." He
flipped his napkin on his lap as the waitress
approached.

Ellie pulled in a breath. No wonder she
wasn't married yet. She didn't know how to

relate to men at all. No matter how the conversation started, she always ended up saying the wrong thing.

They ate their dinners, both managing to get back to light conversation. Since the dinner was a business expense, Cole insisted on paying for her meal, and Ellie just wanted to go home and cry. Could she look any more foolish tonight?

They got into the car, and she finally mustered some courage. "Cole, I'm sorry. I shouldn't have presumed—"

"Yes, you should have."

His words startled her.

"I was out of line. Again. You put me in my place." He turned to her in the darkness. A nearby streetlight revealed only faint images of his face. "Ellie, can we call a truce?" His voice sounded tired.

"I'd like that, Cole."

"Good."

A light rain began to patter upon the windshield. Cole turned and started the car. They pulled onto the road, and he clicked on the wipers. Ellie settled into her seat. The soft whir, mingled with the fine dinner, relaxed her. She closed her eyes and dozed a little while Cole drove her home.

When he finally pulled into her drive, he shut the SUV down and got out before she could. He pulled something out of the trunk and came around to her door. She saw he had an umbrella.

"Thank you, Cole."

"No problem." He held the umbrella carefully over them and walked her to the door.

"I'm glad we got things straightened out between us," he said, when they stopped at the door.

"Yeah, me, too."

There was something in the way he looked at her. "Good night, Ellie."

She gulped just short of audibly. If Cole noticed, he didn't let on. He simply turned and walked away, leaving every nerve in her body on edge. She attempted to push the key into her lock. It took her a full minute to get the door to open. She finally slipped inside.

With a turn of her wrist, she latched the door behind her and leaned against it. What had just happened, she didn't know, but somehow she felt things were about to change.

Ellie hated change.

Over the next few weeks, Cole Preston introduced new procedure after new procedure in office policy. Ellie couldn't understand how Jax could let this man come in and just take over. Pulling up the sleeve of her navy pantsuit, she glanced at her watch. Five minutes until the meeting where she supposed yet another new development would be announced. A bad attitude simmered just below the surface, and she decided she'd better drown it with the only thing that seemed to work for her.

Chocolate.

Pulling a piece of chocolate from her bottom desk drawer, she unwrapped it and plopped it in her mouth. Closing the drawer, she wadded the paper between her fingers and reached for the trash can.

"Pity. I thought you would share with me," a deep voice said within inches of her ear.

Startled, Ellie sucked in a sharp breath, pulling the chocolate to the back of her throat like a dust ball to a vacuum. Gasping for breath and finding none, she panicked. She stood, her arms reaching for something, anything, to find relief. In a flurry of commotion, people called out to her. In that horrific moment, one thought filled her.

Chocolate is going to be the death of me.

Just then, strong arms gathered around her

rib cage. Large fists balled at her midsection and made short, quick jerks until the lodged candy spewed from her mouth like a cork from a bottle.

No one around her uttered a word. Ellie wondered what would be the polite thing to say at a time like this. "Pardon me, I seem to have lost my candy," or, "Yes, would you be so kind as to hand over my chocolate?" Before she could decide, her coworkers patted her condescendingly on the shoulder and went back to work. All but one. The person who had saved her life. She reluctantly turned to see who it was, yet, in the deep pit of her stomach, she already knew. One swivel on her shoes confirmed her greatest fears as she looked into the ultrawhite smile of Cole Preston.

The glare from his teeth gave her a headache.

She swallowed hard, thankful for the ability to do so. "Thank you," she managed with a raspy voice.

"My pleasure—and I'm sorry." His eyes twinkled. He strutted past her and called over his shoulder, "I just had no idea I could choke you up like that."

Ellie stared after the man, speechless. How

could he joke around when she had practically died on the spot?

She glanced across the floor and spotted the offensive little candy that had betrayed her. She ran over, scooped it up in a tissue, and threw it away. How could she face the others in the meeting? A wave of nausea swept over her. Taking a deep breath, she felt her stubborn side kick in.

Placing a legal pad into the crook of her arm, and clutching a pen with her free hand, she pulled her dignity together, lifted her chin and marched straight for the conference room.

He could laugh now, but she'd show him who would have the last laugh.

The entire staff ambled into the conference room, all but Alex who stayed back to man the phones. Coffee mugs lined the table. A box of sugary doughnuts called from the center. Most people gave in to the temptation, while Ellie preferred not to risk another choking hazard. The crowd offered their condolences to Ellie about her little episode before finally settling down to the business at hand.

Coleman Preston stood and welcomed the employees, but Ellie heard very little of his speech. The man drove her crazy, but she had to admit something about him pleased her. Was it his blinding smile, or the way one look into his velvety brown eyes made her feel bundled in a thick fur coat? His wavy dark hair suggested he had had unruly curls as a boy. She wondered if one day his son would inherit the trait. The very thought made her face warm, though a shiver ran through her. She pulled her jacket tighter.

The minutes clicked on in the quiet of the room as workers listened to what Cole had to say. Lack of sleep the night before placed Ellie in a hazy fog, caught somewhere between reality and dreamland. With her left elbow on the table, her chin rested in the palm of her hand. Just as the warmth of the room and the pleasurable rhythm of Cole's voice lulled her to a peaceful state, the word *Ellie* broke through, causing her chin to slide off her palm and her mind to snap to attention. She glanced up to see smiles hiding behind cups and heard a few snickers ripple about the room. Mortified, she looked to Cole, wondering if he had said her name. He had.

And he wasn't smiling.

"I'm sorry?"

"You seem to be having a difficult morning, Ellie. Are you okay?"

Adrenaline pushed her pulse to full speed. "I'm fine. I—I just didn't hear what you said."

"Well, maybe we'll let someone who was listening help us out." Without wasting another breath, Cole moved on.

Ellie felt her knuckles had been sufficiently rapped by that statement. She had been daydreaming. So sue her. His reprimand was all part of his little plan to undermine her authority in the office.

"Which brings me to the most important item on this agenda, and the reason I called the meeting," Cole said.

Uh-oh, here it comes. She braced herself. Cole proceeded to tell the staff Jax had purchased a new computer system. He raved about all the bells and whistles while Ellie felt herself being sucked into a psychedelic black hole, a place where walls spun out of control and the floor rolled and swayed beneath her feet.

Change, change, change.

At the meeting's end, the air snapped with excitement. The room buzzed with comments and laughter at all that the new system could and would do for their company. Ellie didn't want to be a spoilsport, but what was wrong with their current system? It worked for them, didn't it? Why did they have to have bigger and better, as long as they were getting the job done?

She gathered her things from the table and with a heavy heart, headed toward her desk. Her stomach didn't feel so good.

"Hey, Ellie, are you okay?" Jax wanted to know.

She turned. "Oh, I'm fine." She rubbed her temple. "I've just had a rough morning."

"So I've heard," he said with a smirk.

She didn't feel like being the brunt of a joke just now. Throwing him a weak smile, she continued on. He followed.

"I tried to get together with you and tell you about the computer system, but every time I set up a meeting, something came up, remember?"

She nodded. "It's all right." She didn't have the strength to argue. Her stomach rumbled like Mount St. Helens. A queasy feeling followed. Really queasy. "I'm sorry, Jax, I don't feel so good." She dropped her things at her desk and made her way to the bathroom.

Just in time.

# Chapter Five

Cole sat down in front of Jax's desk. "Have you heard from Ellie?" he asked before taking a drink from his coffee mug.

Jax rubbed his jaw. "Yeah, she thinks she'll make it back in on Monday. Her stomach seems finally to be settling down."

Cole shook his head. "She's really had this flu thing bad. I hate that she's had to miss the first week's training on the new computer system."

Jax winced. "I know. This will not be easy for her."

"Because she's hard to train or because she's resistant to change?"

Jax looked up with a start. A knowing smile lit his face and he shrugged. "Both."

"What's up with that?" Cole asked, stretching back into a comfortable position in his chair.

"I don't know. Ellie's always struggled with change. She just likes to keep things on an even keel. When they're not, it throws her into a real spin."

"That's too bad. Life's full of changes."

Jax looked at him a moment.

"What?"

"Oh, just thinking about how you've had to deal with change over your life. Your mom and dad's divorce. Your dad's death. I know it hasn't been easy."

Cole shrugged. "You, too. I mean, with your parents' accident and all."

Jax merely nodded.

Cole thought it best to change the subject. "Hey, did I tell you I rode a dirt bike this past weekend? Now that's a lot of fun. You need to go with me sometime."

Jax shook his head. "You're more adventurous than I am. Parasailing one weekend, dirt-biking, what's next?"

Cole laughed. "I'll think of something."

"That's what I'm afraid of."

Just then Alex knocked at the door and poked her head through. "Ellie's on the phone and wants to know if someone could drop off the new system tutorial this evening?"

"Sure, I'll do it," Cole said, without skipping a beat.

Jax looked at him in surprise. "You don't mind?"

"Not at all. I'll enjoy watching her squirm when I hand her the information."

"You're sad, you know that?"

"Aren't I, though?" He wiggled his eyebrows.

"You want me to tell her you'll stop by after work then, Cole?" Alex asked.

"Yeah, tell her I'll be there." Truth be told, he looked forward to seeing her. The office wasn't the same without her....

Cole pulled in to Ellie's driveway. Cutting the engine, he glanced around the neighborhood. The subdivision was nice and spacious. He hated it when houses stumbled on top of one another. Each lot here had plenty of stretching space. Lots of trees. That was something else he liked. He'd always wanted to live in a house like that, but with his dad's drinking habit and sales jobs, it had seemed they never had enough money. They went from one apartment to the next.

A garage door opened two houses away from Ellie's. A couple of kids stepped through the front door as the father backed the family van out of the garage. An energetic boy bounced a basketball on the driveway, making his way to the car. A little girl with blond, springy pigtails followed, holding on to a pair of skates. The mother appeared with a picnic basket in hand. She yanked the front door of the house to a close, turned to the waiting family, and smiled.

Cole sat transfixed. He wondered if those kids had any idea how lucky they were. What he wouldn't have given for a real family.

How could a mother leave her children, anyway? His eyes glazed over as the image of that long-ago night plagued him once again.

He and his twin brother were doing homework at the kitchen table. Scraps of bologna sandwiches were shoved on the counter with dirty dishes. Cold chicken noodle soup still lined the bowls. His mom stepped into the kitchen with a suitcase in one hand, her face hard as stone. His dad rounded the corner after her, his eyes red and swollen. They were shouting at one another. She stopped when she saw Cole and Caed. His brother had tears streaming down his face, but said nothing. Funny how the images were still so fresh in Cole's memory.

"Where you going?" Cole asked.

"Caed, I can't talk about it now."

"I'm Cole," he corrected her, frustrated that she couldn't get it right. People often confused them since they were identical twins, but he thought their own mother should know better.

Cole jumped from the table and ran to her. He threw his arms around her waist and begged her not to go. She looked at him with a flicker of indecision. He thought he just might change her mind. She scrunched down in front of him and whispered, "Coleman, you take good care of Daddy and your brother, you hear me? You're the strong one." She smoothed his hair from his forehead. "I'll be back and get you one of these days." She kissed his cheek.

He felt as if he'd been punched, the pain spreading all the way through him to his fingertips. He screamed at her, "Mom, don't go!" Ignoring him, she turned and walked out the door to some man who sat waiting in a truck. Cole pushed through the door and ran after her. "Mom! Please, don't leave us!

Don't leave us, Mom! I'll be good. I promise I'll be good." He wiped his face with his arm. "Mom! Don't go!" Why wouldn't she look at him? She got in the truck. The man stared at Cole without expression, pulled the truck into gear, and backed away. Cole's mother never looked up once.

Cole remembered stumbling in the grass and falling to his knees. With the fight nearly gone from him, he had cried out one last time, "Please, Mom, don't go." Tears had blurred his vision as he watched the black truck roll down the street away from him. His body had gone numb. His legs refused to move. How long he had sat there, he didn't know. Finally, he had wiped his face once more on his arm and sucked back further tears, telling himself she'd be back. After all, she had promised.

But Cole never saw her again.

It was after that time that his father started drinking and their lives changed for the worse once again.

Cole's glazed eyes refocused. He wiped the perspiration from his forehead. Taking a deep breath, he picked up the tutorial from his car seat, and headed for Ellie's house.

\* \* \*

A plump lady of about fifty opened Ellie's door. "Cole Preston?" she asked, a pleasant smile on her face.

"Yes."

"I'm Debbie Williams, Ellie's mother." She wiped her hands on her apron and extended her hand. He shook it. "Please, come in," she said, stepping aside. "Ellie will be right in. Make yourself comfortable." She pointed to the tan sofa perched in the living room. "Can I get you something to drink: tea, coffee, pop?"

"I'll take some iced tea if you have it."

"Good. Iced tea coming up."

He imagined she was the kind of woman who felt happiest working in the kitchen. She disappeared into another room while he waited for Ellie. The smell of cooking chicken scented the living room. He looked around. The home had a certain coziness about it. Plump pillows lined the sofa. Pots stuffed with flowers stood near the patio doors. Sensible furnishings adorned the room. Some things looked a little worn. He imagined she struggled to part with anything. Probably had a favorite blanket as a baby. No doubt she still had it tucked away somewhere.

He smirked. He hadn't a clue where any of his baby things were, if they still existed.

"Thanks for coming over, Cole."

He turned to see Ellie standing before him in a pair of jeans, a college sweatshirt and socks. She looked as though she had lost a few pounds. Her chin-length blond hair was parted in the middle, framing her angular face. Her green eyes sparkled, but with a little less luster. She looked cute and perky, like a college student.

"You're welcome. How're you feeling?"

"Much better," she said, sliding into the oversize chair across from him. "I haven't had flu like that since I was a kid."

"Here we go," Mrs. Williams said as she placed the iced tea on the coaster on the coffee table in front of him.

"Thanks."

"You want anything to drink, Ellie?" her mom asked.

"No, thanks."

"Would you care to stay for dinner, Mr. Preston? We're having chicken and noodles, peas, applesauce, pumpkin pie. Nothing fancy, but I'm trying to add a few pounds to Ellie's bones."

He looked at Ellie who blushed at her mother's remarks. "Sure, why not?"

Ellie looked at him with a start.

"Do you mind?" He looked at Ellie then glanced at Mrs. Williams who threw her daughter a you'd-better-be-polite look. He turned back to Ellie who appeared flustered.

"Why, no, we'd love to have you," she all but choked out.

Mrs. Williams snapped her head with approval. "Wonderful, I'll throw in a few more noodles," she said, before disappearing once again into the kitchen. Instantly, he decided he liked Ellie's mother.

He turned back to Ellie. Her weight loss and pink cheeks gave her a sort of vulnerable appeal. He almost wanted to reach over and scoop her into his arms. Almost. Until he followed her gaze to the tutorial. Then another look entirely shadowed her face....

Great. The tutorial looked huge. Just what she wanted, to spend the entire weekend poring over a dull computer book. She felt the urge to run to her bedroom, jump in the bed, and pull the covers over her. Better still, why not grab the chocolate bar in her nightstand and then pull the covers over her?

"Ellie?"

"Oh, sorry."

"I know it looks, well, a little overwhelming—"

She threw him a whatever-are-you-talking-about look.

He pointed. "The tutorial and all."

"Ah."

"It's not so bad. You can call me if you have any questions. I could even come over."

She lifted her chin. "I don't think that's necessary. I'm sure I can handle it."

"I'm sure you can handle a good many things," he said, his eyes glinting with humor.

She wondered what he meant by that. This man could rile her more than anyone she had ever met. Didn't matter *what* he said. It was in the *way* he said it. Oh, she didn't know. She only knew he constantly challenged her Christian walk. She decided to change the subject. "So, how did it go this week at the office?"

Cole swallowed some tea, then put it back on the stand. "Pretty good. I mean, there was the usual groaning and grumbling over learning something new—"

Ouch. He didn't have to say that. Ellie knew that was directed at her. "Well, new computer programs aren't all that easy to learn," she said with a slight snarl to her voice.

"Hold on. No need to get your nose out of joint. I'm just saying—"

"My nose is not out of joint, Cole." Oh, could he ever call out her temper.

He held up his hand. "Look, Ellie, I don't want to upset you." His voice was gentle which calmed her a little. Still, she held up her guard. "I know it's hard to learn a new program. I don't especially enjoy it myself, but I know it will be worth it in the end."

He was right, of course, but she couldn't bring herself to say so. She merely nodded. Sometimes, her own stubbornness frustrated her. Why couldn't she just say he was right? Instead, she fought change with every breath in her.

She felt his gaze upon her, and she didn't like it. He probably thought she was an old spinster, set in her ways. Oh, goodness, she hadn't thought of that before. Was it true?

Just then her mother stepped into the living room interrupting Ellie's train of thought. "I forgot to tell you, your dad called while you were asleep. He'll be here in—" she glanced at her watch "—another fifteen minutes." Before Ellie could comment, her mother disappeared back into the kitchen.

"I like your mom. She's nice."

Ellie smiled. "Thanks." She looked at him a moment. "You know, I don't know anything about your family. Do your parents live in Chicago?" Uh-oh, something in his expression told her she'd struck a nerve. Maybe he preferred to keep his personal life private.

"No. My dad is dead and Mom is, well, I don't know about Mom. I haven't seen her since I was eight."

Shame washed over her. She'd been so caught up in her own stubborn pride at this man getting *her* job, she had never thought about him carrying his own bag of pain. "Oh, I'm sorry, Cole. I didn't know."

He shrugged. "How would you know? Besides, it happened a long time ago. No big deal." He took another drink of iced tea.

"It's a huge deal. Something no kid should have to endure."

"Hey, could I use your telephone? I need to check on something."

His abrupt manner caught her off guard. "Oh, sure." She pointed to the phone on the stand.

He looked embarrassed for a moment. "Could I take this somewhere more, uh, private?"

Now she was embarrassed. "Certainly. The family room is around the corner. Mom's working right next to it in the kitchen, but I can call her out here."

"Thank you. I'd appreciate that."

"No problem."

Cole got up, grabbed the phone, and walked into the next room. Ellie called her mom into the living room. Never had Ellie given thought to the idea that perhaps Cole had a special someone in his life. For some reason, that bothered her a little. Not in a jealous kind of way, of course, but more like a pair of shoes that pinched her toes. It just didn't feel quite right….

Cole stepped into the dark night and made his way to the car. He looked back at Ellie's house and saw her standing in the doorway. She waved. He waved back, climbed into his car, started the engine, and pulled onto the street.

He couldn't deny he'd had a good time with Ellie and her parents. At first, he had felt a little uncomfortable, especially when Ellie had started asking him about his family. At least she didn't have Caller ID, so she wouldn't find out he had escaped her questions by calling Time and Temperature. He smiled.

Still, they were a real nice family. Boy, could they sing! After dinner, they had gathered around the piano and sung together. He'd actually found himself joining in a couple of the old choruses his grandmother had taught him.

Grandma Preston had watched him and Caed when their dad was gone on business trips. He cherished those times with her. Funny, he hadn't thought about that in a very long time. She was the one person in this world he'd felt had really cared about him and his brother. Then she'd died when they were sixteen, and they were pretty much left to fend for themselves.

Cole was older than Caed—only by a few minutes—and had always been the responsible one. He had pretty much taken care of his brother in their growing-up years. Sometimes Caed had resented it, especially as a teenager, but eventually they'd worked through it. Cole was always glad they had each other.

He made a left turn. He didn't like all the memories that flooded his mind today. Sure, some of them were happy memories, the ones with Grandma, but he wanted to forget his past, though Grandma was unfortunately caught up in the mix.

He had a future to make. That's one thing he didn't like about this town. Too much time on his hands. In Chicago, he didn't have time to think. He worked, he played, he worked some more.

This town had a different pace. Too slow for him. He wasn't at all sure this job would work out. He'd get Jax up and running, maybe groom Ellie to take over his position, so he could get on with his life. A life filled with noise and activity. Big-city life.

Yes, that was the life for Cole Preston….

## Chapter Six

Come Monday morning, Ellie felt great. She had planned to start a new diet, some kind of egg diet, but since she'd lost a couple of pounds from the flu, she rewarded herself by packing for lunch a generous helping of lasagna that her mother had brought over.

The weekend was great, too. Though the tutorial didn't answer all her questions, Ellie felt she had learned a great deal from her weekend study. Regardless of what Cole Preston thought of her, she was no dunce.

Reaching for her purse and keys, she went through a mental checklist. Purse, check. Keys, check. Lasagna. Bingo. She reached into the refrigerator and grabbed her pasta container. Stepping through the kitchen door into the garage, she remembered something.

Walking back to the refrigerator, she pulled out the bag holding the garlic bread and stuffed the container and bread in a lunch bag. With a kick in her heels and a song in her heart, she happily made her way to the car.

The sun greeted her as she pulled into the traffic. It promised to be a beautiful summer's day. She switched on her radio, her fingers tapping lightly against the steering wheel as the music bounced through the car. She normally didn't feel this happy unless she was winning the fat fight, but she felt so much better after battling the flu. It was all she could do not to step in an elevator, turn to the strangers on board, and announce with a wide-toothed grin, "I'm all better." Well, why not, that guy on the TV commercial told strangers that his cholesterol was lowered, after all.

By the time she made it to work, her mood had peaked, and she all but skipped her way into the office. She looked around. Too bad they didn't have elevators.

"Well, someone is in a good mood," Cole called behind her.

He must have caught her swinging her purse. She lifted a smile and plopped her purse on her desk. "I feel great. I've got lasagna for lunch—" she patted her lunch bag "—and—" she pulled out her bottom drawer and searched for a moment, then victoriously pulled out a chocolate bar "—this for dessert! What more could a girl want?"

Amusement touched his eyes. "You got me there."

She smiled. Switching on her computer, she stuffed her purse in the bottom left drawer of her desk and looked up to see Cole still standing there.

"Oh, I, uh, just wanted to say, number one, I had a great time with your family on Friday night, and, uh, number two, it's good to have you back."

Speechless, she stared at him. Had he actually complimented her? Who was this man and what had he done with Cole? She got up in his face, as close as she dared, and said, "Is there an alien life-form in there?" She meant to be funny, but when she felt his breath on her cheek, her legs turned limp.

"Has anyone seen Cole?" Ellie heard Jax's voice call from around the corner, bringing them both to their senses. "Oh, there you are," Jax said, looking from Cole to Ellie, then back to Cole. "Did I interrupt something?"

"Oh, no, no," Cole blustered.

Heat climbed Ellie's face. Whatever just happened between her and Cole left her feeling rather unsettled. She watched the guys walk away. Suddenly her giddy mood turned a bit more serious, but something about it felt good. She wanted to linger there just a little while.

By the end of the day, Ellie's mood had taken a definite nosedive. The computer software was giving her fits. She couldn't input anything without causing a major problem, and she had to call Cole every few minutes, which didn't help matters. She hated to admit she wasn't getting it. At least he didn't gloat. If he had shown the slightest inkling of— well, unfortunately, she was discovering she had a dark side.

She had lost count of her trips to the vending machine. Okay, she needed to face facts. One more candy bar, and she'd OD on chocolate. Once again, she was out of control. She blew out a sigh, turned off her computer, and grabbed her purse from the bottom drawer.

"You doing okay?" Cole wanted to know.

Why couldn't he just leave her alone? One minute, he seemed to care as a real friend would. The next minute, he charged through her calm world like hot sauce on a burrito.

"I'm doing fine."

"Come on, Ellie. Work with me here."

She jerked her head to look up at him, surprised by his words.

"I know it's been a tough day. These things aren't easy. We're all struggling, but we'll get through it. You don't have to pretend you've got it all under control, when you don't. None of us do."

"I'm not pretending, first of all. And second, I never said I had it all under control, did I?" She wanted to be stubborn, and yet wanted to give in, all at the same time. This man made her crazy.

He gave a tired sigh and shrugged. "I just didn't want you to feel you were in this alone. That's all." He walked away.

Okay, now she felt horrible. He was kind. She was a jerk. She was the Christian, he was—well, what was he? She didn't even know. One thing she did know, she wasn't representing the Lord very well. With the fire out of her, she picked up her purse and trudged toward her car.

Opening the door, she settled into her seat and took a moment to think. Why did she struggle with change? Some people could just go with the flow, nothing seemed to ruffle them, but not her. When they took her favorite chocolate coffee flavor off the market, she walked around dazed from caffeine withdrawal. She just couldn't make herself change to another flavor. Of course, her love for chocolate won out, and she finally did switch to a new chocolate brand, but not without a bad attitude.

She didn't want to be inflexible, but, well, that's who she was. It wasn't as if she could change herself. It would take counseling. Or, more likely an act of God.

She wanted to relinquish the matter to God, but she was tired and just couldn't think about it. They'd talk later.

For now, she needed to get home and check out the Internet for more information on the egg diet on which Tim Owens's wife had lost fifteen pounds. Ellie would find out what she could and then start it on Saturday. After all, she could handle it. She liked eggs. And besides, things just seemed to go better for her when she had at least *something* in her life under control….

By Saturday evening, Ellie's spirits were better. She decided to hold off on the egg diet until Monday. Why ruin a perfectly good weekend? She had planned to meet her friend, Cheryl, at the Tasty Grounds Coffee Shop, but Cheryl had a sore throat. Ellie decided to go anyway. She hadn't downed a mocha in almost a week. It was time to get one before things turned ugly.

Pulling her car into the parking space, Ellie locked her door and headed for the shop. The rich smell of coffee beans greeted her the moment she stepped inside. Coffee scents were her downfall. Once, she had spotted a mocha candle in a store and purchased it. Every time she burned it, she had to run out and buy a mocha to drink. That candle had cost her a fortune and at least five pounds. It ended up in the trash.

She sucked in another breath. No, it's better to leave the scents here and come visit once in a while.

"May I help you?" the girl behind the counter asked, revealing a crooked smile behind her braces.

Oh, please. The girl looked twelve. Ellie wondered why her town wasn't enforcing the child-labor laws. "I'd like a decaf, skinny mocha."

"It's called 'what's the point?'" the girl said dryly.

Ellie didn't understand.

"What's the point? You know, no calories, no caffeine, what's the point?" she repeated. As in, "duh."

The little twerp. Ellie felt like an eighty-year-old on a restricted diet. "Add some whipped cream," she snapped, showing a spark of rebellion.

Brace Girl smirked and wrote something on a cup, handing it to the next worker in line.

When she received her mocha, Ellie settled into her seat and allowed the rich drink to warm her insides. Though July in Indiana could get quite warm, the wind stirred up a good breeze tonight. The hot mocha tasted good. She gazed out the window. Dark clouds hovered in the distance. Ellie couldn't tell if it was a threatening storm or nightfall on the horizon. Another drink of her mocha made her forget about the weather and nightfall. She just lingered in the moment.

"Well, well, you just never know who you will run into."

Luckily, Ellie had just swallowed her sip of mocha before she heard Cole's voice, or she might have spasmed into another choking fit. Trying to stay calm, she turned to him. "Hello, Cole."

Blinding smile. She couldn't imagine how he could drink coffee and have such white teeth.

"Okay if I sit down?" he asked, cup in hand.

Like she had a choice. "Sure," she said, pointing to the chair.

"I thought I was destined to spend another boring night in Walker, Indiana, but I see my luck is improving." He smiled and took a sip.

Her estimation of him went up a few notches. "Thanks."

"So what are you doing here?"

Ellie shrugged. "I was supposed to meet my friend—"

"Oh," he said wide-eyed, looking around. "He might get upset if he sees you here with me."

Ellie laughed. "No, my friend Cheryl Butler was supposed to meet me for coffee, but she wasn't feeling well tonight. I decided to come anyway."

"Oh, good, I was afraid I had competition." He stared at her.

"Nope." She laughed good-naturedly and grabbed her mocha.

"No competition tonight or in general?" he pressed.

She squinted her eyes. "What are you digging for?"

He shrugged and leaned back in his chair. "Just curious, that's all."

"These conversations always get us in trouble, you know. I've been warned that you're a flirt."

He sat up, feigned shock, then made a face. "Jax ratted me out."

She laughed.

Cole shrugged. "So, do you think I'm as charming as they say?" He wiggled his eyebrows.

She nearly choked on her mocha—which would have been a real waste. Putting her cup down she stared at him, tilting her head this way and that to get a better look from all angles. He squirmed just a tad under her direct gaze. She picked up her cup again. "Well, you maybe have a smidgen of charm about you," she said matter-of-factly.

He sat perfectly still a moment, then seemingly satisfied with that, his lazy grin widened, and he settled back into his chair once again.

She thought a moment. Jax and Alex were

probably out together tonight. She hadn't stopped to consider Cole really didn't know many people in town. When Jax was unavailable, that most likely left Cole pretty much on his own.

"So where do people go around here for fun?" His eyes held a teasing spark.

Ellie shrugged. "Oh, I don't know, there's the neighbor's backyard to watch the fireflies, throwing tin cans at bats and then in July we've got the annual cow-dropping contest."

His eyebrows lifted.

"Yeah, it's as good as it sounds. The winners are the ones with numbers closest to where the cow, um, delivers droppings in the field." She laughed at the face he made.

"You're kidding."

"Cross my heart," she said, drawing an *X* with her finger along her heart. She took a drink of mocha. "Then, of course, you have the usual standbys: movies, restaurants, bowling, shopping, just like most places, I suppose."

"Chicago has its own offerings of city life."

"Oh, Chicago," she said with the air of a socialite, lifting her pinkie finger as she drank from her cup.

"Now, hold on. It's not a slam against Walker. After all, Chicago doesn't have the annual cow-dropping contest, to my knowledge." A smirk tinged the corners of his mouth. "It's just that in Chicago there are plays, big-name stars that come to town, that kind of thing." He took a drink.

Ellie lifted herself up an inch. "Well, why didn't you say so? Walker has a great civic theater. The finest names on the circuit show up at the Walker Civic." She was teasing him now. "There's Penelope Peppers and Petunia, her dancing potbellied pig." She tapped her index finger against the side of her face for emphasis. "And then of course there's Lettie Johnson's juggling act. She's a whiz with tin cans."

He smirked.

"What?" she asked incredulously. "It's a show not to be missed!"

His palm smacked his forehead. "How could I not know that?"

"It's beyond me."

"Maybe you'd like to take me to what's playing, say, next Saturday?"

Uh-oh, now he was going too far. So much for keeping things on a professional level. Still, she couldn't deny the compassion and, really that's all it was, that tugged at her heart at his solitary state.

"But, of course, if you're ashamed—"

Oh, smooth, she had to give him that. "I'm not ashamed, I just don't know if it's a good idea for us to be seen together, um, in that way."

"Two friends going to a show is wrong around here?"

"Well, no, it's not that—"

"Okay, what is it then?" His eyes challenged her.

Oh, she hated it when he trapped her like that. He hadn't meant it as a date, of course, still it would look like a date. But then she couldn't say that, because she would be "assuming," and she'd already made that mistake in the past. "Nothing," she said with defeat.

"Great. Find out what time the show starts next week, and I'll pick you up."

"You're something else, you know that?"

"Oh, you ain't seen nothing yet," he said with a wiggle of his eyebrows.

Ellie couldn't help but laugh. Before they knew it, they were knee-deep in talk of work and some of Cole's past work experiences, which Ellie had to admit she found fascinating.

"Hey, you two," Brace Girl called.

They looked up with a start.

"Notice anything?" she asked, making a sweeping gesture of the room with her hand.

"Oh dear, are you closed?" Ellie asked, glancing at her watch.

"No, we're not closed, but the place cleared out because there's a tornado warning for this area."

"Tornado!" Ellie squeaked the word. "What are we going to do?"

Brace Girl had nerves of steel. "My boss says we have to go in the bathroom till it blows over."

Ellie stared at her, willing herself to breathe.

Cole grabbed Ellie's arm. "No problem. Any chance we could get a couple of frappecinos while we wait?" he asked with a wink.

"As a matter of fact, I just made two frappes and one latte. The two frappes were for customers who left before I finished making them. The latte is for me." She flashed her braces.

"Great," he said, helping Ellie to her feet.

"I'll get the drinks. You grab the radio off the counter, and we'll all meet in the ladies' restroom," Brace Girl said, practically breathless with excitement.

Why were they acting as though they were going to a party? Didn't they know how dangerous tornadoes in Indiana could be?

Cole could feel Ellie's arm trembling beneath his fingers as he escorted her to the ladies' room. A reaction to the storm, no doubt. She must have a past history with tornadoes. Though she drove him crazy most days, he couldn't help wanting to protect and calm her just now. They had that sort of push-pull relationship.

"You okay?" he asked Ellie once he helped her sit on one of the chairs he brought into the room.

Not looking at him, she nodded. He reached for her hand. "Ellie, everything will be okay."

"I know. I'm fine," she said, lifting her head to look at him. Her voice and her eyes told him otherwise.

"Here we go," the employee said, bringing in a tray of drinks with all the grace of a perfect hostess. She passed them out, then scrunched down to turn on the radio.

The trio listened, quietly sipping their drinks, while the announcer told of fallen trees, downed wiring, scattered debris.

"Looks like we'll have to stay put awhile,"

the girl said. "By the way, I'm Amy," she offered with a smile.

"Hi, Amy. My name is Cole, this is Ellie."

Ellie raised her head and smiled. "I can't believe we're sipping frappes in the ladies' room while a tornado hurls overhead. Kind of gives a whole new meaning to swirlies." She smiled.

Cole laughed. "You mean where bullies at school dunk your head in the toilet and flush?"

She giggled and nodded.

"Don't tell me you ever had one?"

"No. I was just hoping I don't get one tonight." She glanced over at the toilet and pointed toward the howling winds overhead.

Cole threw back his head and laughed some more. "Leave it to you to think of that!"

"I had a swirlie once," Amy said. "I thought it was kind of cool."

Ellie and Cole exchanged a glance and laughed. Amy joined them.

Just then Amy got a call on her cell phone. She went into the men's restroom for privacy to talk.

"So you want to tell me why you're especially afraid of tornadoes?" Cole probed.

"Oh, it's nothing."

"Come on, Ellie. Something happened to you as a kid." His voice was soft and kind, seeming to offer just the encouragement she needed.

"We were at church. Dad was leading the music when someone ran into the church and screamed, 'Tornado!' I was about six at the time."

Cole nodded.

"A loud sound, like a train, blared outside just before a huge wind pushed inside and forced my dad to the floor. In an instant, I screamed and Mom yanked me down under a pew with her. I closed my eyes, and held my hands hard against my ears. Mom held me tight while I wailed. I thought we were going to die."

Cole watched her relive the past. He wanted to reach over and pull her into his arms, shield her from the memory.

"I don't know how long we stayed there. I just remember when we finally got up, everything was deathly quiet. When Mom helped me from under the pew, I heard her gasp. Wallboard, plaster, debris everywhere. Fortunately, all the people had gathered under pews, so it didn't look as though anyone was hurt. But then we looked on the platform where Dad had been standing. It was destroyed." Ellie took a deep breath. Cole reached over and rubbed her hand.

"It's okay, Ellie, you don't have to talk about this if you don't want to."

"No, it's all right. I heard Mom scream his name. Everyone started searching and there he was at the end of the church, rolled up in the carpet! He later told us when the tornado hit, it uprooted the carpet, causing him to fall right into it. The carpet rolled down the aisle with Dad inside." She laughed. "It's funny now, but at the time, I was terrified." She grew serious. "They told us the carpet saved his life." Reaching over, she grabbed some tissue and wiped her eyes. "We knew God had spared him."

"Wow. That's some story, Ellie." Cole squeezed her hand. "No wonder tornadoes frighten you. I'm sorry."

She shrugged. "I can't hear about tornadoes without thinking of that night. Truly, it turned out to be a night of thankfulness. Miraculously, no one was hurt. Of course, our church was ruined."

Amy stepped back into the room. "It was my mom checking on us. She said the tornado has moved on, so it looks like the worst is past. We just have to be careful going home. Don't go near the power lines."

"Good advice, Amy. Thank you. Do you get to close shop now?"

She nodded. "My boss said when the threat was over, I could close the store."

"Is your mom picking you up?"

"No, I drove."

Cole looked surprised.

"I know, everyone thinks I'm twelve, but I'm really twenty-two."

Ellie coughed.

"We'll stick around till you get everything done, and see you out to your car."

"Thanks."

"What do we owe for these frappes?" Cole asked.

"They're on the house," she called over her shoulder, already preparing things to leave.

"You want me to follow you home, Ellie, just to make sure you get there safely?"

"That's not necessary, Cole."

He shrugged. Knowing how independent she was, he didn't want to push the matter. They threw away the coffee cups, gathered their things and headed toward their cars.

After saying goodbye, Cole climbed into his SUV and started the engine. Only after pulling into traffic did he realize he actually had a "date at the theater" with the elusive Ellie Williams.

## Chapter Seven

Grabbing her Monday-morning coffee, Ellie headed for her desk.

"I guess you heard the news?" Cole said with a bit of a bark to his voice.

"Good morning to you, too, Cole." Ellie tossed a half smile and settled into her chair. She thought the least he could have said was that he'd had a nice time at the coffee shop Saturday night.

"Well?" He raised his hands, palms up.

"Well, what?" she asked, only slightly paying attention as she glanced through a file.

"Have you heard the news?"

"No, Cole, what news?" She really didn't feel like playing this game. And she definitely didn't like the edge to his voice.

"The tornado did extensive damage to the three homes in Woods Edge. Ripped roof sections off two of them, broke some windows, stripped off siding."

She closed the file and looked up with a start.

"The one we started last week has to be totally reframed," he said, clearly frustrated.

Ellie gasped, pulling her hand to her mouth.

He looked satisfied with her reaction. "Good thing we're insured. Still, it's going to put us behind in our deadlines. It will take a lot more effort on our part to get things up to speed."

Terrific. He was stressed. She knew what that meant. More changes.

"I'm sorry, Cole. Is Jax okay?"

"Oh, sure, Jax is fine. He doesn't want to deal with this. He—" Cole looked around. Ellie followed his gaze to see sales associates Tim Owens and Chad Brunner listening in. "Come to my office."

Ellie grabbed a legal pad, pen and her coffee cup, then followed him to his office. Cole waited for her to step inside. He closed the door behind her. "Sit down, Ellie," he said, nodding toward the chair.

She complied.

Cole walked over behind his desk, sat in his chair and began cracking his knuckles, a sure sign he was upset. She watched him for a moment, waiting for him to say what was on his mind.

"Look, Ellie, I know you and Jax are good friends. Jax is my best friend, but the truth of the matter is, Jax wants out of this business. We both know that. He doesn't want to deal with the tough things. That's why he hired me." He worked on a knuckle that refused to pop. "To tell you the truth, I don't know that I want to handle this."

Interesting situation, she thought. Here he was pouring out his troubles to her, a mere employee, and he the partner of the firm. She stopped her prideful thoughts. "What do you mean by that, Cole? Are you wanting to quit?"

His head jerked up. "No, I'm not a quitter," he said, his voice sounding offended. "But I hadn't expected Jax to 'check out'—" he said, using air quotes, "—so soon."

"Well, he hasn't exactly checked out, has he? I mean, he's still around most of the time."

"True, but in body only. He sits in his office and studies for his classes. He leaves the decisions up to me, handling only the phone calls he's forced to handle."

"Well, after all, Cole, you did agree to be his partner." Her voice sounded a little colder than she had intended. Was she basically saying, "You made your bed, now lie in it"? She knew she should feel ashamed, but there was a teensy bit of "na-na-na-na-boo-boo" going on in the darkest corners of her heart.

He glared at her. "Thanks for the reminder."

Against her better judgment, she went soft. "I'm sorry, I just don't know why you're telling me this. I mean, what do you want me to do?" Sounded to her like Cole and Jax needed to talk things over.

"I don't know," he said with a sigh. "I'm not one to give up on a project without seeing it through to completion—"

She threw him an oh-really look, which he didn't miss. He held up his hand. "I know I have a reputation for having a commitment problem, but I do see my projects through to completion. I *am* professional." His tone was slightly defensive.

She shrugged, a smile tugging at the corner of her lips. For the life of her, she tried not to enjoy this little moment of having the upper hand, but she couldn't help herself. He was the partner, but he was asking her for advice. She settled into her seat, sipped from her coffee cup, and decided this particular Monday had definite potential.

"But I'm a little frustrated by his less-than-enthusiastic contributions to help me. I know he's anxious to do the school thing, but I feel as if he's dropped his baby at my doorstep and walked away."

"I still don't know why you're telling me instead of Jax."

He stared at her a full moment. "You're right. I need to talk to Jax. I guess I just needed to vent to someone else first, and well, you're the one who came to mind."

She smiled, sort of. An uncomfortable feeling settled upon her. After all, Jax was her friend, and Cole, well, she wasn't sure what he was, but she was sure she didn't want to get in the middle of something between the two of them.

"Talk to him, Cole. But don't worry about the houses, we'll be all right. We'll just put the appropriate people in place and get things moving."

"Ellie, I don't think you're taking this seriously. We have contracts. Due dates on those homes. We have to get them finished. On time. Do you understand that?"

Okay, now he was getting her dander up. Seems he had a knack for that. He obviously thought she had dismissed the whole matter too easily. "Cole, I think I can understand that. I've been in this business awhile, even though you think I'm not capable of handling—"

"Look, Ellie, this is not about you. This is about—"

"Who said it was about me?" She rose from her chair, chin lifted a notch.

"Now hold on. Sit down, Ellie."

Just who did he think he was, ordering her around? She swallowed hard. Oh, yeah; he was her supervisor. Reluctantly, she settled back into her chair.

"I don't mean to argue with you. I just mean—" he ran fingers through his hair "—I don't know what I mean."

So the mighty partner was stumped. What was the big deal? They were under a time constraint. She had dealt with those before. It wasn't the end of the world. "We'll get through it. Don't worry." She tried to make her voice gentle and encouraging, but she wanted to bonk him on the head. Men could be so stubborn. She felt a prick to her conscience. Okay, so she could be stubborn, too, but she didn't want to go there just now.

She stood to her feet. "Talk to Jax," she said as she walked across the room. Before closing his office door, she glanced back. Cole stared out the window, his brows drawn together, chin resting in the palm of his hand.

Her insides went soft. Again.

Two days later, Ellie noticed Jax in his office. A textbook was opened in front of him on the desk. She decided to stop and say hello; she hadn't talked to him in a while. "Got a minute?"

He glanced up, and a smile lit his face, his shoulders relaxed. "Sure. Come in," he said, stretching back in his chair and yawning.

"Studying hard, huh?"

He nodded and thumped forward in his chair. "I've forgotten how tough it is to be in school." He rubbed his eyes then looked at her. "So, how's it going?" Before she could answer, he continued, "I'm sorry I've been kind of scarce these days."

She waved off his comment. "No problem. I understand you're working hard with school and all. I just wanted to see how you were doing."

He nodded. "Thanks. It's going pretty well." He told her about his classes, discussing the challenges of going back to school.

After some small talk, she stood to go. "Well, I don't want to keep you. Just wanted to say hello." She walked toward the door and turned back to him. "By the way, sorry about the houses, but I don't think it will be a problem to get them up and going again."

"The houses?"

"Yeah, you know, the ones in Woods Edge that were damaged by the tornado."

He looked as though he'd just been doused with cold water. Uh-oh, she hoped she wasn't out of line. "I'm sorry, Jax. I thought you knew." She walked back over and sat down.

Jax blinked his surprise. "No, can't say that I did. I mean, I knew about the tornado and that it hit that side of town. I just hadn't considered it hit our houses. Now I understand why Tim and Chad got quiet when I walked in on them talking about it. I just didn't get it. Wonder why Cole didn't tell me."

She stammered. "Well, he's been working

hard to get the matter taken care of. He probably didn't want to burden you with it," she said, meaning it.

He seemed to consider the information and rubbed his jaw. "How bad are they?"

She did not like the way this discussion was going at all. She'd assumed Cole had talked to him. Well, maybe Cole would appreciate her softening the blow. Besides, Jax had a right to know. This was his business after all. She explained the extent of damage.

"I still can't figure out why Cole hasn't told me," he said, clearly perplexed.

"Look, Jax, he's been really busy working—"

"Still." He rubbed his jaw some more. "I don't like being kept in the dark about things."

"I'm sure he was trying to spare you while you're busy with school."

He looked at her a moment, then his face brightened. "Yeah, you're probably right. I just don't want Cole to think I'm not available, and well, I'm not ready for him to take over entirely just yet. I have school bills to pay."

"I don't think he wants to do that."

"I'd better go talk to him."

She thought a moment. "He was going to the Barnes' job site, and said he'd be back this afternoon. Besides, you'd better let him come to you. I don't want him to think I was going over his head or anything. I just assumed he had already talked to you."

Jax looked down at the pencil he tapped nervously on his desk. "I'll give him till tomorrow," he finally said, looking up.

Ellie nodded and stood to her feet. "Well, I'd better get back to work," she said with more calm than she felt.

"Thanks, Ellie."

She smiled, but her stomach felt as if she'd been to an all-you-can-eat burrito buffet. Stepping out of Jax's office, Ellie turned in the hall, nearly running into Cole. "Oh, hi." One look at his hardened face and angry eyes told her he wasn't feeling sociable.

"You want to tell me what that was all about?" he asked, folding his arms across his chest.

Had he overheard them? "I don't know what you mean, Cole," she answered, mad that her voice was trembling.

He tugged her arm, edging her farther down the hall, away from Jax's door. "What did you talk to him about?"

She felt herself tense. Boy, try to help somebody and all you get is heartache. "Look, Cole, I thought you had told him about the houses—"

"I didn't," he groused.

"Well, I found that out after—"

He smacked his forehead. "Great. Just great." He glared at her. "I don't believe you! I take you into my confidence, and you go running off to tattle the first chance you get."

Her jaw dropped. "I was not tattling! I thought you had told him. *Any* rational person would have thought the same. I was just assuring him the matter was taken care of."

"I don't need you, Ms. Williams, to back me up. I can stand on my own, thank you very much."

"I was trying to help."

"Don't do me any favors." He looked so deep into her eyes, she thought he'd bore a hole through her head. "Next time, I'll be more careful in choosing someone to talk with." He turned to go.

"Oh, Mr. Preston, about the theater?"

He turned back around to face her.

"I won't be going."

* * *

Ellie adjusted the earpiece to her cell phone and started her car engine.

The phone rang twice. "Hello?"

"Hey, Cheryl, do you have a minute?"

"Sure, I'm on lunch. What's up?"

Ellie could hear Cheryl unwrapping her sandwich. "Tuna salad today?"

"No. I splurged. Roast beef sub. And before you say anything, I've been good for the past two days, so I've earned it—and the candy bar."

Ellie laughed. "I'm not one to cast stones, believe me. If someone would come up with a chocolate diet, I'd be their poster child."

"I hear ya," Cheryl said as mannerly as possible while chewing her sandwich.

"Listen, I had to talk to someone. Cole is making me crazy." Ellie waited for Cheryl to finish chewing. She thought a moment how thankful she was to be able to spend time with her best friend. She could talk to Cheryl about anything. Last year, when Cheryl had decided to attend night classes after her day job as a paralegal, they had hardly seen each other. So when Cheryl had announced school was not for her, though feeling a bit selfish, Ellie was relieved.

"Him again? What's up with you two? One minute, you're friends, the next minute, well—" She stopped and Ellie could hear her take another bite.

"Oh, I know it." Ellie turned left at the traffic light. "I messed up big-time today. I didn't mean to, though."

"Uh-oh, doesn't sound good. Want to meet for coffee tonight?"

"Could we? I really could use someone to talk to."

"You got it."

"Will Mark mind?" Ellie asked, though she knew Cheryl's husband probably wouldn't.

Cheryl took a drink of something. "Sorry," she finally said. "No, he won't mind. He has a church board meeting."

"Oh, great. Meet you at six-thirty, Tasty Grounds?"

"See you then."

Ellie clicked off her phone, thankful for a friend who was always there for her.

After picking up their coffee, Ellie and Cheryl made their way to the table.

"Mmm, I love this place," Ellie said.

Cheryl smiled. "Yeah, me, too. And to think I didn't even drink coffee until they started with all the flavored stuff. Now, I'm a caramel latte junkie."

"Tell me about it. Who would have thought chocolate and coffee would fit like tea and sugar?" Ellie laughed before taking a sip of her mocha. "I say chocolate plus anything equals a delightful experience."

"You should do a commercial. And speaking of delightful experiences, you want to tell me the problem with you and lover boy?" Cheryl's eyes twinkled.

"For crying out loud, Cheryl, don't call him that," Ellie snapped.

Cheryl raised an eyebrow. "My, we *are* a little touchy."

"Oh, I'm sorry. The man drives me nuts, and he's not my lover boy!"

Cheryl shrugged. "Whatever you say."

Ellie looked at her in disbelief. "How can you say that, Cheryl? You know he's practically fingernails on a chalkboard."

"Precisely my point."

Ellie stared, saying nothing.

"Look, Ellie, Mr. Right isn't going to be perfect. You're always looking for someone without any flaws. If he was out there, Hollywood would have a reality show about him."

"What got us into Mr. Right? We're talking about Cole Preston making me crazy."

"Exactly."

Ellie was not enjoying this conversation.

"I'm sorry, Ellie. It just seems so clear to me that you're attracted to him and that's why he drives you crazy."

"You can't mean that."

"Think about it. I know his little quirks bother you, but those same things about him make you dig deeper into yourself. It's like he's exposing you to yourself, do you know what I mean?"

Ellie rolled her eyes. "You take one class in psychology and you've been analyzing ever since. I need a friend here, Cheryl, not a shrink." Normally, Ellie could handle Cheryl playing Dr. Phil, but not tonight.

Cheryl shrugged and took a drink of her latte.

Ellie leaned into the table. "Look, Cheryl, I'm sorry. I just want to know how to work with the guy without losing my mind. Can you help me with that?"

Cheryl noticeably softened and nodded. "Just promise me I'll be a bridesmaid."

Ellie groaned.

## Chapter Eight

The next couple of weeks passed in a blur. Ellie kept busy with new clients, and Cole got the house repairs underway so they would be back on schedule soon. They had apologized to one another over their latest tiff, though they still kept their distance in the office. Ellie finally got a break from Cole's upheavals and yet she felt strange about it all. She couldn't quite put her finger on it.

Maybe Cheryl had been right. Oh, not the attraction part, but maybe Ellie liked the fire that sparked between her and Cole, the challenges he hurled her way. She couldn't imagine what would make her think such a thing. She hated changes. And *change* was Coleman Preston's middle name.

"You coming, Ellie?" Her mom and dad

stood at the church doors, holding them open for Ellie as she lagged behind. She quickened her pace.

"Sorry, Mom."

Her parents smiled at her, then they walked into the church foyer. They greeted their church family and when Ellie turned to her right, her heart seemed to stop midbeat.

"Hi, Ellie," Cole said, standing a short distance away. He fingered his collar and adjusted his tie as she walked toward him.

"Cole," she said, ignoring the continuing leap in her pulse. "Nice to have you join us this morning." She surprised herself by meaning it.

"Thanks." He flashed her the blinding grin. "Jax made me come."

They both turned to Jax who had just finished talking with someone and turned back to them. "Hey, Ellie. Guess you see who I forced to come this morning," he said, giving Cole a manly pat on the shoulder.

"See what I mean," he said to Ellie. Turning to Jax, he said, "Come on, I'm not that bad. I've been to church before."

Jax and Ellie stared at him, both of them grinning. "Well, I have. Grandma used to take me and my brother all the time."

They laughed out loud. "We believe you,

Cole," Ellie said, feeling kinder toward her supervisor than she had in weeks. The worship team started singing, and Ellie turned to walk with her parents. "Hey, Ellie, why don't you sit with us?" Cole asked, surprising her.

"Well—"

"Come on, sis," Jax chimed in, using the nickname he used only when away from the office.

Cole looked at him. "I didn't know you were related."

Jax shrugged. "Well, technically, we're not. But I've taken it upon myself to take care of her. So you'd better behave yourself. Big brother is watching."

Cole threw a mock salute toward Jax and the three made their way into the sanctuary. They settled into their seats with Ellie sitting in the middle.

The first service was more of a contemporary nature, with lively, upbeat music. Jax and Ellie clapped their hands in beat and sang along heartily. Cole shifted uncomfortably from leg to leg, looked around, and shifted some more. Ellie pretended not to notice. She wanted to make him feel comfortable, but he didn't know the songs, and she didn't know what to do. After a little while, she saw him mouth the words on the overhead screen and attempt to join the rest.

Following the morning greeting where people sitting nearby extended a welcome, the congregation sat down and prepared for the message. Ellie prayed a silent prayer for Cole. She had not been a good example of Christ to him and guilt plagued her for that. She didn't want to be the reason someone else stumbled in their relationship to Christ.

The pastor spoke about control. How we need to give our lives over to the Lord, allowing Him full control of our lives, our dreams, our future. She wondered if that was a little heavy for Cole, but figured the Lord knew what He was doing.

The Scripture reading was from Proverbs 3:5-6, talking about trusting in the Lord and leaning not on our own understanding. Ellie was quite familiar with that verse; it was one of her favorites. She shifted into a more comfortable position in her seat, preparing herself for a good message. But as time lingered on, she noticed her back was getting sore. Her left leg went to sleep. She could feel a headache coming on. To be honest, she didn't like where the pastor was headed with his sermon. She had relinquished control of her life to God, so why did she feel uncomfortable? She couldn't quite put her finger on it, and quickly shoved it aside. Besides, she needed to pray for Cole. As far as she knew, he didn't know the Lord. This was about him. Not her.

Cole listened intently to what the pastor had to say. Did people really do that, surrender their lives, their wills, to someone unseen? He couldn't do that. Oh, sure, he believed in God. After all, Someone had to create everything, but this yielding control business bothered him. Seemed more like a crutch to depend on Someone other than himself in everyday life. He figured it was enough to visit God on Sundays and maybe have a slight conversation throughout the week. But the business of building your world around Him, that didn't set well with Cole.

He stole a sideways glance at Ellie. Then Jax. They seemed engrossed in the message. He appreciated his friends and felt sorry he couldn't share their beliefs. But this was a free country, and a day of tolerance. They could each believe their own way without affecting the other.

After church, Ellie's mom walked over to them. "Jax, how about you and Cole joining us for lunch?"

"Oh, I wish I could," Jax said, glancing at his watch, "but I'm supposed to pick Alex up in a half hour. We're going on an afternoon picnic."

Cole was surprised to hear that. Jax had said things were getting strained between him and Alex.

Mrs. Williams frowned then turned to Cole. "How about you, do you have plans for the afternoon?"

Cole had no idea how to get out of this, and Jax looked as though he enjoyed watching Cole squirm. "No plans, ma'am."

"Good." She glanced over at Ellie and smiled. Ellie's face had turned a pasty white. He wasn't sure if he liked having that effect on her. Not that he cared one way or another how Ellie felt about him.

Oh, he liked her as a person, as far as that went, but anything beyond that, he wouldn't begin to entertain the thought. She was too stiff for his tastes. Didn't like adventure or change. That spelled boring in his dictionary. Looking at her once more, he couldn't deny she was pretty, present paleness notwithstanding. At first glance, he would definitely be attracted to her, and come to think of it, he had been. In the beginning. Before their obvious differences sent up red flags.

Okay, so he was still attracted to her. But he wouldn't allow his emotions to overcome his good sense.

"Cole?" Jax tugged at Cole's arm.

"Oh, sorry," Cole said, embarrassed he had been caught daydreaming.

"I said I'll see you later. Try to get along with Ellie for the sake of her family, okay?" Jax's eyes held a teasing glint.

"How could you think otherwise?" Cole acted offended.

"I'll just let that one go by. See you later, buddy," Jax called over his shoulder.

"You want to follow me to my parents'?" Ellie asked.

"Sure."

"It's only a couple of miles down the road."

"Don't you have to come past here to go back to your house?" he asked.

She nodded.

"Well, why don't you leave your car here and ride with me? I'll drop you off on our way back."

He noted her hesitation. No doubt she felt as nervous as he did about this whole thing, but still it seemed the logical thing to do. What's a couple of miles in the car together?

"Okay, that will be fine, I guess."

"I won't bite, I promise."

"So you've told me," she answered dryly.

"And?"

"And what?"

"Have I kept my word?" He rather enjoyed the bantering.

She waited, squinted her eyes and looked toward the ceiling. Finally, she looked at him. "So far, so good."

His head snapped in an I-told-you-so fashion. "Let's go."

"Great meal, Mrs. Williams. Thank you for saving me from a lunch of canned ravioli."

Ellie's mom laughed, her slightly plump middle shaking a tad. "Glad you could join us, Cole. You're welcome to come over any time."

Ellie winced. She could tell her mother was on a mission, and Ellie didn't like it. They'd talk later.

"Excuse me, where's the bathroom?" Cole asked.

"Down the hall to the right," Ellie said, pointing.

Cole nodded and left the room.

"Mom, please, don't encourage him," Ellie whispered, emphasizing each word. "He's my boss, and I don't want to pal around with him." She helped her mother clear the dishes from the dining room table.

"Now, Ellie, I'm merely extending a Christian welcome to the young man. 'Whenever you do it unto the least of these,' remember?" Arms full, they carried the dishes into the kitchen for washing.

Ellie groaned. "Do you have to bring God into everything, Mom?"

Mom shrugged. "He is in charge of my life. Controls every aspect." Ellie could almost see her mother in a spy suit, peering over the rim of her dark glasses, eyes boring into the secret places of Ellie's heart.

Ellie squirmed. "And that's another thing. Why do you always try to apply the pastor's message right after service? I'm not five anymore, Mom. I get it, okay?" Ellie tried not to show her frustration, but for crying out loud, her mother had been applying the morning message right after church for as long as Ellie could remember. Her mother used to say, "If you apply it right away, it will stick in your memory longer."

"Just trying to be a blessing, dear," her mother teased.

Ellie wasn't amused. In fact, her mood was growing downright bitter. Cole's presence made her uncomfortable. Mom's mission made her nervous, and for reasons she couldn't explain, she didn't like the pastor's message. "Where's your chocolate stash?"

"Oh dear, I've upset you," her mother said, reaching for a candy bar.

Ellie sighed. "I'm sorry, Mom. I'm just a little on edge." She unwrapped the chocolate bar and took a bite.

"Why?"

"Different reasons. Cole's requiring more documentation of our client interaction and—"

"Hey, nice pictures in the hallway," Cole interrupted when he came into the kitchen.

Ellie jumped. "Thanks."

"A lot of them have you holding a book or something. What's that about?" He directed the question to Ellie, but her mother dove in with the response.

"Oh, Ellie struggled each time her dad moved to a new church, so she found comfort in her journals. She's kept every journal she's ever written since she was seven," her mother said, puffing up with pride.

Cole looked impressed.

Ellie inwardly groaned, took another bite of her candy bar, and headed for the living room. Her mom stayed behind to finish up in the kitchen. Her father had had to go back to the church and find some music.

"What was that about?" Cole asked when they sat down on the couch.

Words bunched in her throat. "In case you haven't noticed, I don't like to talk about me," she said when she finally found her voice.

"I've noticed. So what was that about?" he repeated with a grin.

She made a face.

"Must have been hard."

"What?"

"Moving all those times when you were a kid. Adjusting to new schools, new friends. Some kids do okay with that, some kids don't. It's a personality thing."

Ellie nodded and kept chewing. She wished everyone would leave her alone so she could enjoy her candy bar.

"I didn't move a lot, but Dad was always gone on business trips."

Ellie stopped chewing and looked at him. He rarely talked about his personal life, and when he did, she listened.

"We had Grandma, and I loved her, but it wasn't the same as having Dad around. Sales work was all he knew, and he had to put food on the table." Cole shrugged and paused a moment. "Dad was good at it, too, until the booze took over."

Her pulse gave an unexpected blip, taking her breath away for a moment. She couldn't believe it. They were actually having a serious conversation, looking into each other's hearts. Well, she was peeking into his anyway. For some reason, that made her very uncomfortable, and yet, on the other hand, she felt strangely warmed by it all. The strains of "Kumbayah" returned in a faint whisper, startling her.

He straightened himself and stared once again into the distance. "Dad sure knew how to have fun. The adventurous type, you know?"

She nodded. "Like father, like son?" she asked with a smile.

"Yeah, I guess so," he agreed. "Dad, my brother and I, we did all the manly things. Fishing, hunting, scuba diving, you name it."

He stopped again. "Until he started drinking."

"I'm sorry, Cole."

He shrugged. "You know, he hardly ever drank until Mom left." He shook his head and turned to her. "Good grief, I'm telling you my life story. Sorry."

"It's okay."

"Let's talk about you."

"Let's not."

He ignored her. "I can understand why you struggle with change. You want to avoid it because it makes you uncomfortable, makes you think of your childhood days of upheaval."

For crying out loud, first Cheryl, now Cole. She was surrounded by amateur therapists. "Don't tell me you just happened to bring the ink blot test?"

He held up his hands. "Okay, okay, you win. I'm out of line here. But if you ever want to talk, I'm here for you," he said with a wink.

She finished her candy bar.

Cole's cell phone rang. "Hello? Yeah, uh-huh. When?"

Ellie could tell something was wrong by the frown on Cole's face.

"I'll be right there." He folded his cell phone. "I've gotta go," he said, rising to his feet.

"What's wrong?"

"Vandalism at the Shady Acres job site."

She groaned.

"We can't afford this right now," he said, walking toward the door. "We're going to have to make some changes." He stopped at the door. "Can your mom drive you back to your car?"

Ellie nodded.

"Sorry to do this." He blew out a sigh. "Tell your mom I said thanks for dinner." Cole turned and walked out the door.

Ellie watched him. "Great. More changes." She sighed, then looked at the candy wrapper in her hand and wadded it up. Time to start a new diet....

The next morning, Cole came charging into the office like a bull moose at a Victorian tea. "We're going to have to keep a tighter rein on these subcontractors, Ellie. They're getting lax at putting away supplies. Things are getting stolen. We've got to let them know we mean business."

"Good morning to you, too, Cole," Ellie

said, trying desperately to stay calm. "I see you've had your coffee already," she said dryly, clicking on her computer and forcing herself to present a calm demeanor. Maybe it would help him.

It didn't.

"Good morning. And yes, I've had my coffee. Did you hear what I said? We need to crack down on those guys."

"I heard." She grabbed her coffee cup. "May I?"

He frowned. "Yes." He followed her to the coffeepot. "I mean it, Ellie. We can't afford the time these set-backs cost us."

He didn't have to tell her that. She was upset about it, too, but it wouldn't help matters if they were both stressed about it.

She nodded and poured her coffee. Pulling some hot chocolate from the cupboard, she added a spoonful of chocolate to her coffee and stirred. She turned to him. "I understand."

Cole gaped at her. "That is just gross," he said, looking at the chocolate globs in her cup.

She stirred them away. "It's chocolate and coffee. You ever heard of mochas?"

He clamped his mouth and glared at her.

"You do understand then?" he asked, returning to the matter at hand.

She took a sip. "Yes, Cole. I'll look into it. What else do you want me to say?"

"Well, it would be nice if you took something seriously for once," he snapped.

"I don't know what you're talking about, Cole. If you think I'm not doing my job, tell me. Don't beat around the bush."

"I just wish you'd show a little concern when I stress the importance of things. I might as well be telling you about the weather."

Her temper pushed all thoughts of calm aside and shot to the forefront. "I'm not like you, Cole," she hissed. "I," she said with emphasis, "handle things differently." Her chin lifted with an air of piety.

"That would explain some things."

She stiffened. "What is that supposed to mean?" Her face felt hot, burnt-toast hot.

Morgan and Chad walked within earshot. Cole closed his mouth and pushed out a heavy sigh. She half expected to see smoke come from his nostrils. "Nothing. Nothing at all." He turned and walked away.

# Chapter Nine

"Jax, I can't do this," Ellie said, struggling to stay seated across from him.

"What's the problem, Ellie?"

"Cole Preston, that's the problem. He is impossible. I can't work with him." Her words were punctuated with anger, and she didn't care. She'd had enough.

"I know he comes across a little bossy—"

"A little? He acts as though he's the only one who knows anything around here. I didn't exactly start this job yesterday, you know." She stood and walked over to the window.

"Listen, Ellie, you need to calm down."

She spun around to look at him, wanting to deck him for keeping his nose in a book. "You don't know how it is around here, Jax.

You've been busy." She measured her words evenly.

"Busy, yes. Blind, no. Now, sit down."

His voice took on an authoritative tone, grating on her raw nerves. She took a deep breath to calm down. "Can't you get rid of him?" Guilt called to her, but anger chased it away.

"No, Ellie. I need him. I need you both."

Her lips pressed together, and she lifted her chin. "I have to go. I have an appointment." She stomped toward the door.

"Ellie?"

She turned around.

"I'll pray about it. You do the same, okay?"

She turned and yanked the door open. Her thoughts whirled with her emotions. *I don't want to pray about Cole. I don't want to pray about my attitude. As a matter of fact, I don't want to—pray.*

Practically on the heels of Ellie's departure, Cole stomped into Jax's office. "Can we talk?"

Jax closed his textbook with a sigh. "Come in, Cole."

"I can't work with that woman," he said just as the door closed.

Jax held up his hand. "Don't tell me, let me guess. Ellie, right?"

"The woman is unteachable. She's resented me from day one." He thumped toward the window. For a moment, he stared out the window then whipped around to face Jax. "You have to get rid of her. I can't work with her."

"Now, hold on, Cole. I need her. I need you both."

Cole grunted. "I'm going to lunch early," he announced, not caring what Jax had to say....

Cole visited job sites all afternoon, and that allowed Ellie the time she needed to cool down. By the time she arrived home, she was ready for a walk. Donning her sweats and reliable gym shoes, she headed toward the river walk. Only two streets over, the path for walkers was a convenient way for Ellie to exercise. The walk always cleared her mind and helped her relax.

She felt herself calm the moment she started the trail. What had gotten into her today? Cole had gotten her back up instantly, as he had since day one, and she couldn't imagine how her insecurities had brought her this far. After all, she resented him for getting the partnership. She held on to that resentment like a pit bull with a chunk of beef. Why?

*Lord, what is wrong with me? Cole is a nice man. Why do I struggle with his authority? I resent his position. I'm jealous, inflexible, and basically a jerk apart from You.*

Ellie kicked a scrap of bark from her path and wiped the tears that escaped down her cheeks.

*Help me to see Cole as You see him, and help me to submit to his authority as my supervisor. Most of all, may he see less of me and more of You in me.*

By the time Ellie had worked through her prayer and made her one-mile trek, her heart felt much lighter. Thoughts of the pastor's message surfaced. One thing at a time, she told herself.

Once home, she took a shower, ate dinner and settled into a good mystery. The phone rang beside her, making her jump.

"Hello?"

"Ellie, this is Cole."

She took a deep breath. "I'm glad you called."

"You are?" The surprise in his voice made her smile.

"Yes, I am."

"Why?"

"I want to apologize for my behavior. I can't promise I won't struggle with your authority from time to time, but I can promise that I'm working on it and, with the Lord's help, I'll do better in the future."

Silence.

"Cole?"

"Yeah."

She liked the sound of his voice, deep, masculine.

"Are you okay?"

He chuckled. "Yeah, I'm okay."

She heard him sigh.

"Look, Ellie, I called to apologize to you. Seems we do this a lot."

"I know," she whispered into the phone.

"I wish we could just erase everything and start over. I have a feeling things could be very different between us."

She didn't even want to think about what that meant, and she tried to ignore the way his words soothed her ruffled nerves.

More silence.

"Well, uh, I just wanted to set the record straight."

"Thanks, Cole."

"Um, I don't suppose you—?"

"Yes?"

"Oh, never mind. See you tomorrow, Ellie."

"Okay." Without thinking, she cradled the receiver in her hands for a full minute. She made an audible gulp. "What in the world has gotten into me," she said to her living room. She got up from the recliner and walked to the kitchen for a drink of water. Only then did she see her hand trembling.

Cole stared at the phone. A simple conversation, but somehow it left him shaken. The sound of her voice, sweet, vulnerable. Was that Ellie? Maybe he'd called the wrong number. She was clearly changing, despite her protests to the contrary.

What about you? The thought came to him out of nowhere. He pondered it a moment. He supposed he could stand to change some. Okay, maybe a lot. But that's not something a person can do by himself.

He thought some more. Ellie had said, "With the Lord's help." Did she really believe God could change her like that? Isn't God too busy running the world? He mulled the idea over in his mind. It just didn't set well with him. His grandma had believed that—and she was a saint if there ever was one—but he couldn't help but feel that a real man handled things himself. And that's what he was, a real man.

Just like his dad.

He shook his head. He might as well face it. A real man would have left the bottle alone and helped his kids get through a tough world without a mom. It takes a real man to accept failure and grow from it. Everybody reaches for something to get them through the tough spots. His dad took to alcohol. Cole worked his frustrations out with new adventures like dirt bikes and parasailing, among other things. Ellie—he smiled—worked through her struggles with chocolate and/or diets. He shook his head. Seemed like an oxymoron to him, but then she could be that way sometimes.

Not that adventures and chocolate were bad. What mattered were the motives behind them. His motive for keeping every minute occupied with some new thrill, new challenge. Ellie's motive behind the chocolate binges. He looked at the ceiling. *Are You trying to teach me something here?*

It took a moment to digest everything. Maybe he needed to talk to Jax. It didn't hurt to find out more. He smiled at the thought. He'd better break it to Jax gently. Once Jax heard Cole was interested in knowing more about God, the man would probably keel over. Hadn't Jax been trying for years to talk to him about such things, but Cole had always shrugged it off? Not this time, though. He wanted to know.

The phone rang. Cole got up from his couch and walked over to answer it. "Hello?"

"Hey, Cole."

"Yes? Do I know you?" Cole teased, knowing full well it was his brother.

"Okay, so it's been a while. I've been a little, well, busy."

"With the women, no doubt." Cole had missed their banter.

"Guilty as charged."

Cole laughed. "So, how's it going?" Cole asked, walking back to the couch and settling in for a good talk.

"Pretty good. I've been offered a job and I've accepted it. I'm going to finalize plans before moving."

"Really? Tell me about it."

"It's a law firm in southern Indiana. Pretty reputable firm, looks like a good opportunity.

I've quit my job here, and I'm taking a month off to relax."

Cole nodded. He knew his brother had been in a tough job, working as a lawyer and a public defender in Chicago. He'd suffered burnout and needed some time to heal his tired body and mind.

"Sounds like a good plan, Caed."

"My appointment is the end of August. I thought if you didn't mind, I'd come and stay with you for a couple of weeks before it."

"What? That would be great! Let's plan on it."

"Really?"

"Absolutely. I miss you, little brother."

Caedmon laughed. "You just can't let go of the fact you're a couple of minutes older than me, can you?"

"Nope."

"Well, you'd better watch yourself. I'm as big as you, you know."

Cole groaned. "Yeah, I know."

"So, how do you like living in Farmsville?"

"Oh, that's cute. Real cute. Actually, it's not half bad. I mean, the people are friendly, the job is fine, my coworkers are, um, interesting."

"What does that mean?"

"Let's just say life is a little slower-paced here than in Chicago."

"I'll bet," Caed said with a laugh. "I'm thinking that's how it will be where I'm going. But to tell you the truth, I could stand a slower pace right now."

"Yeah, I know it's been a tough couple of years for you," Cole agreed.

"I decided if I wanted to live to see my children grown, I'd better find another job."

"Whoa! Children? Did you say children? I didn't think we'd been apart that long."

Caed laughed. "I mean future children. Nothing in the works."

Cole let out an audible sigh. "You had me worried there for a minute."

"How about you? Anyone special in your life right now?"

Cole paused, though he wasn't sure why. "No. No one special."

"Hmm, that didn't sound very convincing. Are you sure?"

"I'm sure," Cole said quickly. The last thing he needed was for Caed to start in with his matchmaking schemes. Sometimes he wondered who parented whom between the two of them.

The two brothers talked awhile longer,

each sharing a little of what had been going on in their lives since Cole had left Chicago.

"Well, I'll plan on getting there next Thursday, if that works for you," Caed said.

"What time? I need to make sure I'm off work and not on an appointment."

"I'll probably arrive around four or so. I know you're not home by then, so I'll just look around the area, maybe even stop in at your office."

"Sounds good. I'll plan to be home by five if I don't see you before then."

"Okay, big brother," he said, emphasizing *big*.

They both laughed. "Can't wait to see you, Caed."

"You, too."

Cole hung up the phone. It would be great to get together with Caed. They hadn't really had much of a chance to talk. It would be good to catch up on things.

Cole held the phone a moment. Before he lost his nerve, he punched Jax's number, then took a deep breath.

"Hello?"

"Hey, Jax. Glad you're home."

"I'm not getting rid of Ellie," Jax said in a

definite I-don't-want-to-talk-about-it-any-more tone.

Cole laughed. "Sorry, guess I made you a little edgy, huh? I'm not calling about that."

Jax hesitated. "You're not?" His voice perked up considerably. "What's up?"

"Since you don't have class tonight, I wondered if you had time to go for coffee?"

"Well, sure." Jax sounded as though he could use a little company himself. "When and where?"

"Tasty Grounds, in a half hour?"

"Okay, I'll see you there."

That's what Cole liked about being a guy. When guys decided to get together, they could do it on a whim. It seemed women had to plan things weeks in advance or it threw their whole world into chaos. He'd just never understood that.

Cole hung up the phone, his heart thumping. He wasn't sure where this all would take him, but this time, he was willing to find out.

Not wanting to appear too anxious, he turned on the news for a minute to kill some time. An advertisement flipped on about an antique car show. Maybe he'd take Caed over there. His brother had always had a taste for old cars. He might enjoy it. Besides that, what else was there to do in Walker, Indiana? It certainly didn't offer what Chicago did, but he had said he wanted a change of pace, and Cole figured Walker would offer that very thing.

Cole rubbed the back of his neck. He couldn't imagine people actually settling in a town like this. He supposed it appeared desirable to Caed because of his burnout at work. Cole wasn't sure he could settle anywhere, let alone a quiet little town far from the big-city lights to which he was accustomed.

He stretched and yawned. Not that it mattered. He didn't have a reason to settle down anywhere. Jax had known the risks when he took Cole on at the office. It was a trial thing. Cole would stick it out for a while, but, well, he just couldn't see himself staying around. Life had too many things to offer. People to meet, places to go, adventures to experience. He'd just help out his college buddy for a while, then be on his way.

With a glance at his watch, he decided it was time to go. He grabbed his keys and headed for the car.

Jax and Cole sat at the table with their coffees in hand, the no-frills, thick black stuff.

Cole figured real men drank espresso—or practically as strong—the kind of brew that grew hair on your chest and made you want to yodel and swing from a tree. Jax was a little more tame, using a swig of cream, but he argued he could beat his chest with the best of them.

"So, you gonna tell me what this is all about?" Jax asked, taking a gulp of his drink.

"Can't a guy ask his bud to coffee for no reason?"

Jax shook his head.

Cole shrugged. "Okay, you found me out. I have some questions, and I thought you'd be the best one to answer them."

Jax raised his eyebrows. "Uh-oh, sounds serious. Work-related?"

"Nope."

"Really?" With eyes narrowed, Jax stared at Cole. "Now I'm puzzled. I can't imagine what I could give you advice on. You're the expert."

"No. No, I'm the jack-of-all-trades, master-of-none, remember?"

"Well, I'm not a master of anything, either."

"Ah, but you know the One who is."

Jax looked at him, hard, as if he hadn't heard right. "What are you saying, Cole?"

"I'm saying all these years you've been trying to talk to me about God, and I wasn't interested. Well, now I'm interested."

Cole thought that if Jax's eyes got any bigger, they'd pop right out of his head.

"Well, for the first time in my life, I'm speechless."

Cole laughed. "We can wait a minute. If I know you, it won't last long."

They spent the next couple of hours discussing God, His truths, His Word, the misunderstandings of man, the things yet to be revealed.

"Wow, you've given me a lot to digest," Cole finally said.

"Listen, Cole. I have an extra Bible at home. How about I bring it to work tomorrow, and you can take it home. I'd like you to read the Gospel of John in the New Testament. Start tomorrow reading the first chapter. Call me with any questions."

Cole nodded. "I don't know how I feel about it all just yet."

"I understand," Jax said. "But God is working on your heart, Cole. Give Him your full attention before you make your decision, okay?"

Cole nodded. "Thanks, Jax. You're a good friend."

"I'm just glad you talked to me about this. I'm telling you, Cole, I've never regretted my decision to follow Him."

"I believe you. There's a difference in your life. In Ellie's, too. I mean, you're both human, make mistakes, but there's still that difference. And that's what I can't get away from."

"I'll be praying for you, man," Jax said, as they walked toward their cars.

"See you tomorrow, buddy."

Jax waved.

Cole climbed into his SUV and started the engine. *"Thanks,"* he whispered into the night air, feeling sure Someone had heard him.

## Chapter Ten

At the Chinese restaurant, Cheryl and Ellie followed the waitress to their table.

"So, Ellie, how was work today?" Cheryl asked, as the waitress seated them. The scents of Chinese cuisine hovered over the nearby buffet table. "Mmm, that smells good enough to eat."

"Call it a lucky guess, but I think they planned it that way," Ellie said. She glanced at the table, squinting to see what was there.

"You gonna get the buffet?" Cheryl asked.

"It looks good, but I'd better not. I shouldn't eat that much."

Cheryl smirked. She started to comment then seemed to think better of it. "So, you didn't answer my question. How was work today?"

"Oh, it was fine." Ellie looked around at the oriental decor and noted the music playing softly overhead. She could kick herself for never learning to use chopsticks.

"No problems with lover boy—I mean, Cole?"

As if Cheryl had happened upon Ellie's chocolate stash, Ellie pinned Cheryl mid-breath with a don't-even-think-about-it glare. Before Cheryl could comment further, the waitress walked up and took their drink orders.

"Seriously, I'm going to work through this, Cheryl. I've been praying about the situation, and I think it will be okay." In hopes of dismissing the matter, Ellie opened one of the menus the waitress had left. "I'm starved."

"Well, now, there's a surprise."

Ellie made a face.

"Which diet are you on today?" Cheryl asked, glancing through the list of entrées.

Ellie winced.

Cheryl put her menu on the edge of the table and leaned forward. "You know it's a control issue, don't you?"

Oh, no, Dr. Phil came to dinner. Ellie knew she might as well not fight it. She put her menu down and looked at Cheryl. "Control?"

She said the word with a definite, do-tell sound to it.

Cheryl nodded. "It's a food issue. You feel like your life is out of control and food is the one thing you can control, so you diet." Cheryl leaned against the back of the booth looking rather intelligent.

"You're saying it's bad to want to control my food intake?"

"Dieting is not a bad thing, if you're doing it for the right reasons. You know, health problems and all."

"So, are you going to have me on your TV show, Dr. Phil?"

"Go ahead and make fun," Cheryl said, sounding smug. "I'm just trying to help."

"I thought mother hens protected their chicks, not pecked them to death. Between you and Mom, I feel like hanging out with a fox would be safer."

"Any fox I know?" Cheryl raised her eyebrows.

Ellie pulled her mouth into a thin line.

"Okay, okay, I'll behave." The waitress placed their drinks in front of them, and Cheryl took a sip of her iced tea. "But I still think you should consider what I said about the diet thing. I mean, if you were truly serious about dieting, you wouldn't hoard chocolate. We both know you don't need to diet. And if it's a control thing, well, we know Who is supposed to be in charge."

Ellie wasn't in the mood for a sermon. She snapped open her menu once again. "Can we change the subject?"

"Sure," Cheryl replied pleasantly. "Just remember, best friends say the hard things."

That's why so few people have best friends, Ellie thought, though she kept the comment to herself. For the flit of a second, she wondered if what Cheryl had said was true. After all, chocoholics and dieters really didn't mix. Why did she diet? She always blamed it on weight, but deep down, she knew her weight didn't fluctuate all *that* much. She just needed a reason to diet. Oh, she hated it when Cheryl was right. Not that she was convinced that Cheryl was right on this matter. At least, not yet. Ellie decided maybe she'd think about it later. Maybe.

In a weird sort of way the conversation actually lightened her mood. She could forget her liquid diet and eat whatever she wanted tonight. And right now, fried rice, egg rolls and assorted entrées, topped off with fortune cookies, sounded pretty good....

* * *

The next morning, Ellie called a couple to set up an appointment to go over floor plans. After contacting a few subcontractors about a current job and then documenting tasks completed in her file, she took a breather. Making circular motions with her shoulders, she tried to work out the kinks. Her muscles could knot up faster than three chili dogs in an empty stomach. She rolled her head from side to side.

"That bad already?"

Cole stood beside her, grinning.

"Hi," she said with a smile. She told him what she had been working on.

"Hey, listen, I've been thinking."

Uh-oh, never a good sign when Cole had time to think.

"I thought it would be a good idea if on the day we are scheduled to visit job sites, we do it in the mornings from now on, rather than the afternoons." Before she could respond, he continued, "That way, we could make the necessary phone calls for those particular homes in the afternoon when we returned to the office."

She swallowed hard. "That's fine, Cole, if that's what you want to do." She smiled, though she mentally tried to work through her schedule to accommodate the new policy.

His eyes narrowed. "Excuse me, but do I know you?"

"Okay, so I'm not the most flexible person around."

Cole simply laughed and walked away.

Staring after him, she couldn't decide whether she liked him or not. Her mother's words from long ago came back to her. "Eat your oatmeal, Ellie. You will find life is not always the way we want it, but some things you just have to endure."

She smiled to herself. That pretty much summed up her relationship with Cole Preston.

He was like oatmeal.

And her family knew that oatmeal was one thing Ellie Williams could live without.

Cole's legs felt like dead weight as he walked out to his car. It seemed everyone wanted to buy a home and have it built before the cold weather set in. Once inside his car, he glanced at the time. Caed should be getting to his house any minute, if he wasn't already waiting. Cole backed out of his parking spot and glanced over to see Ellie walking out the door. He waved at her.

Pulling into traffic, he thought about her a

moment. He had to admit their working relationship was improving, though at a snail's pace. Despite the changes he implemented, Ellie didn't seem to buck him as much as before. No doubt about it, she was changing. He could only pray things continued to run smoothly.

Pray. Now that's something in which he had little experience. Still, he had to admit he was learning from his study of John. Jax met him on Thursday nights to talk over any questions or comments. Though Cole continued to have lots of questions, he couldn't deny his longing to know more about the God whom Jax and Ellie served.

Rounding the corner toward his house, Cole saw a car in his driveway. He smiled. Once he pulled into the garage, he got out and walked toward the other car. A man stepped out.

"Hey, big brother," said Caed, pulling Cole into a bear hug.

After the hug, Cole studied him. "You know, it's kind of scary how much we're even aging alike. Same dark eyes, our hair's still the same color, height, weight—it's still like looking in the mirror."

Caed shrugged. "Oh, come on, admit it, I

have better hair." He ran his palms along the sides of his hair for emphasis, then laughed and swung at Cole playfully.

"It's a matter of opinion," Cole said with a laugh, dodging Caed's punch. "So, you need help with your luggage?"

"Sure." Cacd opened the trunk of his SUV and pulled out a small suitcase and garment bag. Cole crooked the garment-bag hanger on his fingers and whisked it over his shoulder.

"Did you have a nice trip?" Cole asked as they stepped through the garage into the back of the house.

"Yeah, it was okay." They walked through the kitchen and into the living room. "Not bad," Caed offered, looking around.

"Thanks. Your room is back here." Cole led his brother down the hall and opened the door to a bedroom. Once Cole had shown Caed around, they sat at the kitchen table and ate ham sandwiches and chips. They talked about their lives over the past few months, catching each other up to the present.

"So, do you have feelings for her?" Caed asked, after Cole discussed his job and coworkers.

"No, she's Jax's woman."

"I wasn't talking about her. I was talking about the other one."

"Oh, you mean Ellie?"

Caed nodded and grinned.

Cole held his hand up as if to stop his brother's thoughts. "No possible way. She's a nice woman and all, but she's definitely not my type."

Caed's eyebrow spiked. "Really?"

"Really," Cole said with a little impatience. "That woman rattles my nerves." He shook his head. "We do what we have to for survival, but that's about it. Why do you ask?"

Caed shrugged. "You just mentioned her a lot."

"That's because we work closely together."

Caed studied him.

"What?"

"Um, I don't know. There's just something in your voice."

"Look, little brother, Ellie Williams is nice. But she's not at all my type."

Caed whistled. "How so?"

"I like adventure. She likes—well, I don't know, she's boring."

"That bad?"

Cole nodded.

"So, are you going to tell me?" Caed pressed.

"Tell you what?"

"What she looks like?"

"Hey, why are we discussing Ellie? I work with her. We do what it takes to get the job done, end of discussion. Now, tell me more about you." Cole wanted to make it perfectly clear that he didn't want to discuss Ellie Williams. His brother seemed to pick up Cole's irritation and changed the subject.

After they'd been talking a little while, someone rang the doorbell. Cole walked over and opened the door. "Hi, Jax, come on in."

"I knew Caed was coming, and I thought I'd drop in and say hi."

"Come into the living room. We're just sitting around shootin' the breeze."

Caed glanced up, then stood, saying "Hey, Jax!" and the two hugged. "Wow, it's been a while since I've seen you."

"Yeah, it has."

The guys spent the next hour catching up on things, until finally Jax glanced at his watch. "I guess I'd better go. I'm supposed to meet Alex for coffee."

"So how are things going with you two?" Cole asked.

Jax waited a minute and sighed. "Not good."

"Really?"

"She's getting too possessive, and I'm growing very tired of it. I mean, she is nice and all, but well, it's just not there for us."

"Uh-oh. Are you going to tell her?"

Jax frowned and nodded. "I'm afraid so. We're going to dinner tomorrow night, I thought I would do it then. There's not enough time to talk things through tonight."

"Oh, wow. That's tough," Caed said.

"Does she have a clue?" Cole wanted to know.

Jax shook his head. "I didn't decide it myself till recently. I sat down and really thought about it and realized this wasn't the direction I wanted to go. I had to be honest with myself, and now I need to be honest with her."

Jax stood to go. The other two followed him to the door. "Let me know how it goes, buddy," Cole said.

"You interested in her?"

"No way. I don't want to deal with that on top of everything else in the office," Cole said.

"Everything else, as in Ellie Williams?"

Cole nodded.

Jax grinned. "I don't know what to do with you two."

Cole glanced at Caed whose expression said he had a secret. "What's the matter with you?"

"Oh, nothing," Caed said with a grin.

His brother had been home only a few hours and already Cole wanted to deck him. This reminded him of their younger days. The last thing Cole wanted was for Jax to get the wrong impression of his feelings for Ellie.

"Am I missing something?" Jax asked.

"Yeah, your coffee date if you don't hurry," Cole said, practically pushing him out the door. "What are you doing?" Cole asked Caed once he closed the door.

"Nothing." Caed headed back to the living room.

"Look, Caed, I love you, man, but please don't get into your matchmaking mode again, okay? If I meet someone I'm interested in, I'll let you know. Until then, just enjoy your vacation, and let's have a good time, all right?"

"Sure," Caed said, but somehow Cole felt

he was being patronized. "Want to have lunch tomorrow?"

Cole shook his head. "I can't. I have to meet with some contractors at a job site. In fact, I've got several appointments tomorrow. Be out most of the day."

"Maybe you can take me to the office on Saturday," Caed mentioned.

"Sure, that would be great." Cole looked at his brother's expression a moment. He didn't like what he saw there. Something about Caed's expression spelled trouble. Cole inwardly groaned. They had been through this so many times before. To pay Cole back for his help in their younger days, Caed's goal in life was to find Cole a good woman. Not just any would do. She had to pass Caed's approval. Cole glanced at his brother again. Uh-oh, Cole had seen that look before. Caed was on a mission, no doubt about it. Why didn't Caed just push him over a cliff? It would be easier on everyone.

Caed tossed him a broad grin.

Yep, Cole thought, his brother was up to something. It was as sure as death and taxes.

## Chapter Eleven

The next day at work, Ellie made her way to the refrigerator for her salad. Cole had told her an hour ago he was leaving for an appointment, yet when she walked by his office, he was still there. She backtracked.

"Hey, I thought you were leaving."

He glanced up. "Ellie?" He said her name as if he had no clue who she was.

"Are you okay?"

He smiled so big, she could have stuffed a banana in his mouth sideways.

It irritated her a little. "Well, did you call the Kennedys? I mean, weren't they expecting you?"

He seemed flustered. "Oh, that, uh, yeah, I talked to them. In fact, it was their idea to cancel. Yeah, that was it. They couldn't make it." He fidgeted with a folder on his desk.

Ellie stared at Cole. He was acting very strangely. Her gaze ran over his shirt and tie and black pants with a sharp crease down the center of each leg. How odd. Cole never fussed with creased pants, and almost always wore jeans on days he visited job sites. Her eyes narrowed. Something seemed very odd about him today.

He glanced back up. "You need anything else?"

She snapped out of her mental wanderings. "Oh, no. Nothing."

"Well, I guess I'd better get back to work," he said.

Feeling a tad embarrassed by his dismissal, she mumbled, "Oh, sure." She started to walk away when she heard him say her name.

"Ellie?"

She took two steps back and stopped in front of his door. "Yeah?"

"You look great today."

She was stunned into silence. That didn't happen often. Okay, try never. "Thanks," she finally managed.

Another smile. She turned away and continued on toward the kitchen.

No question about it, she could not figure him out. One minute he upset her, and the next, he said something that took her breath away. Trying to understand Cole Preston was near to impossible.

Still, she couldn't deny she rather liked it when he was this way. In fact, she could almost pretend it was worth wading through his not-so-pleasant ways. Namely, changes.

She reached into the refrigerator and got her salad, then went back to her desk. Pushing thoughts of Cole aside, she decided to check her e-mail while she enjoyed her lunch. Cole had sent a message. Uh-oh, probably another change.

Hope you didn't mind my forwardness just now. But I couldn't help but notice how your blue jacket made you look so vibrant. My tongue got away from me. Sorry. But what can I say, you sort of took my breath away.
Cole.

She stopped chewing her carrot in midbite and stared at the screen. A couple of more chomps, and she swallowed hard. Her eyes scanned the e-mail once more. Then again. One more time for good measure.

Waiting a minute, she looked away from the screen and rubbed her eyes. She glanced around the room to see if anyone was watching her. Morgan sat at her desk, staring into her own computer screen. Tim and Chad were out on calls. She peeked back at her computer screen, half expecting the message to be gone, a figment of her imagination.

There it was in all its glorious color. Well, okay, black print on a white background, but still. She checked the name of the sender. *Cole*. She re-checked who it was to. *Ellie*. She reread the last line, her eyes emphasizing the final phrase, *...you sort of took my breath away.*

*Sort of,* as in not really, but kind of did? Meaning, she didn't really take it away, but then again, she sort of did.

Suddenly, she felt a little giddy, as if she'd downed a double shot of espresso. With trembling fingers, she reached into her bottom drawer to pull out her stash of chocolate and celebrate. The bag was gone! Had she eaten all of it? She didn't remember. Thrashing through her drawer, she pulled out files, papers and debris, until finally, hidden carefully back in the corner away from the files, she glimpsed a wrapped piece of chocolate.

She gave an audible sigh. Carefully unwrapping the tasty morsel, she plopped the candy in her mouth and felt better instantly. Don't try to analyze the compliment, she told herself. Enjoy it. He thinks you look nice. Period. She glanced at her clothes. Pastel blouse, light blue jacket, and matching skirt. She'd have to remember that. Not because of Cole, exactly, but a girl liked the idea of being noticed by members of the opposite sex. Even if they happened to have a toothless grin and only five long hairs stretched across their head.

But, of course, that hardly described Cole Preston.

Ellie glanced at her desk calendar and shook her head. Friday. Where had the week gone? It had seemed to fly by as she'd put together some house deals and worked like crazy to close on pending sales. She and Cole had run into one another on occasion, but he seemed swamped with his work, too.

What she couldn't get over was the change in him. She felt as though she had stepped into a fairy tale where she was the princess. He opened doors for her, complimented her, went out of his way to do special favors, and even brought her chocolate from the Sweet Shop down the street.

Feeling sure he was preparing her for a huge change, she kept waiting for the news to hit. But it never did. The way Cole had changed toward her made her want to change all the more.

She smiled. God was working in her life and she was changing. Something that did bother her a little, though, was how Cole's new behavior affected her. There was a stirring of something deep down inside her. Maybe it was just the extra pepperoni on last night's pizza, but she didn't think so. And at present, she didn't want to know.

They weren't fighting, and that was enough for now.

"Hey, Ellie, these came for you. I'm green with envy," Alex said, placing a vase of colorful flowers on her desk.

"Wow. I can't imagine. It's not my birthday or anything." Ellie picked at the card, feeling a little nervous that Alex was waiting for her to open it. Maybe her parents thought she needed a little encouragement. She'd been complaining a lot lately.

Her fingers trembled as she worked the flap of the tiny envelope. Finally, it flipped open and she pulled out the card.

"What does it say?" Alex said, clearly excited over the whole matter.

"It says—" Ellie stared a moment, then glanced back at Alex.

"Well?"

"It says, From Your Secret Admirer."

"Well! It must be nice!" Alex said in a snooty voice before turning on her heels and heading back to her desk. Ellie wondered what that was all about and figured things must not be going well with Jax and Alex.

Ellie turned her attention back to the card. *Secret Admirer.* For a fleeting moment she wondered if Cole could have sent them. She shook her head. True, he was being nice lately, but she couldn't imagine him going this far. Oh, well, it was kind of fun having a secret admirer. The very idea held a certain amount of charm.

"Hey, Ellie, just thought I'd let you know, I'm headed over to the Wilson job site. You want to come along?" Cole asked.

"No, I've got some paperwork I have to get through, if that's okay."

"Sure. It actually works out well. I have

other appointments outside the office scheduled today. Since I don't have to bring you back, I'll probably be gone until about three o'clock or so. Just so you know." He paused then glanced at the flowers. "Wow, where did you get those?"

He looked genuinely surprised. Her spirits plunged. Okay, so he hadn't sent them. But who then?

"Well?"

"Um, a friend sent them."

"Really?" His eyebrows raised. "Looks serious."

She barely lifted the corners of her mouth in a smile.

"You okay?"

"Sure, why?"

"Oh, I don't know, you're just acting funny. Does it have something to do with the flowers?"

"No." Obviously a friend had sent them. An enemy wouldn't have. It was none of his business anyway.

"Your left eye always twitches a little when you're upset or trying to hide something, did you know that?" He pointed his finger within inches of her eye.

"Stop that," she said, pushing his hand

away. Cole's laughter floated after her as she stomped to the bathroom. Oh, he made her so mad. If he were an egg, she would have beaten him.

She didn't like teasing. Especially from him. What did he care who sent her flowers? It's not as if she owed him an explanation anyway.

In the bathroom she took a moment to calm herself. She did not want to give him the satisfaction of seeing her upset. She reapplied her makeup and after she'd settled down, peeked through the door. No sign of Cole. She stepped through and tiptoed back to her desk.

By early afternoon, Ellie was so engrossed in her work, she had forgotten the entire incident.

"Hi, Ellie. Nice flowers. Who's the secret admirer?"

Her head shot up. Cole had changed clothes. "You read the card that came with them?"

He held his palms up, facing her. "No, why?"

"Why did you say that?"

"Say what?"

"Oh, nothing. Forget the flowers. We've already had this discussion."

"Sorry, just wanted to say they're nice," he said in a soft voice, making her feel guilty.

"Look, I'm just a little touchy after this morning."

"What happened this morning?" he asked.

Boy, sometimes she just didn't get him. The past week, he had been acting so weird. "Never mind." She studied him a moment. "I thought you weren't coming back until three o'clock?" Her eyes narrowed. "And why did you change clothes?"

He looked down. "I didn't chan—" He stopped himself. "Oh, that." He shrugged.

She eyed him with suspicion. "Well, people don't usually go home and change clothes in the middle of the day," she probed.

"Spilled coffee on my shirt."

"I thought you had given up coffee—well, at least the coffee in the office. Said it wasn't any good, remember?"

He coughed. "Oh, uh, I did, but—" He gave a sheepish grin. "Well, what can I say? I needed caffeine and, um, I caved."

"You know, Cole, you've been acting strange lately. You feel okay?"

"I'm fine. Couldn't be better," he said, a touch overenthusiastically. "Uh, Jax wanted to see me, I'd better go." He walked away from her.

"Cole?"

He turned around. "Yeah?"

"Jax's office is that way," she said, pointing in the opposite direction.

He smacked his forehead with the palm of his hand. "Oh, yeah. Right." He walked past her and headed for Jax's office.

Something very strange was going on with him. And Ellie intended to find out what it was.

That night after dinner, Cole and Caed settled down to watch TV. Caed picked up the remote.

"Before you do that, Caed, we need to have a talk."

"Uh-oh, I don't like the sound of that. You're using your big-brother voice."

"You want to tell me why you've been slipping into the office while I'm out and pretending to be me?"

Caed feigned innocence. "What are you talking about?"

"Don't give me that. Jax told me. Ellie talked to him about how strange I had been acting lately, sending her e-mails, saying things I don't normally say, that kind of thing. She wouldn't give Jax the details. You want to fill me in?"

Caed sunk further into his chair. "Um, not really."

Cole glowered. "I think you'd better."

"Well, good grief, Cole, you wouldn't know a fine woman if she had a seal of approval stamped on her face."

"I knew it," Cole said, slapping his knee. "You're trying to set us up! I don't believe this. I don't even want to think about what you've done, Caed. How can I look Ellie in the face again?"

Caed leaned back into his chair. "I've done you a favor."

"I'm in no mood for this, Caed."

"Okay, so I've maybe stepped over the lines, but—"

"Stepped over the lines, is that what you call it? Brother, you're way out of bounds! You deceived her, making her think you were me. How do you think she's going to feel when she finds out the truth? She'll feel stupid, that's what." He got up and started pacing. "No one wants to look like a fool."

"I wasn't trying to do that, Cole. Honest. I just know you have feelings for her, and I was trying to let her know that in a subtle way. And I was trying to get you to see the truth."

Cole jerked around and pinned Caed with a glare. "I don't have feelings for her!"

"Yes, you do."

"Cut it out, Caed."

"It's the truth."

"You know nothing about me and women!"

"I know you're in love with this one," Caed pressed.

"I've never loved any woman!" Cole said through clenched teeth.

"Well, now you do."

"I do not!" Cole stepped within inches of his brother, feeling as though he might clobber him.

"You call out her name in your sleep."

Cole felt like he'd been doused with ice water. It took a full moment to find his voice. "So what, people can't help what they dream," he snapped.

"You fell asleep on the couch while I was watching TV. I had just turned it off and you kept saying her name."

"Probably because I thought we were at work."

"Look, you weren't speaking with your professional voice."

Cole didn't even want to know what that meant. He took a deep breath. "My subconscious was goofing around with you, then," Cole hedged. "I know how you get all caught up in that stuff." His mind raced to distract Caed. Otherwise, Caed would run with this.

"That's not even possible, Cole. You might as well face facts. Whether you like the idea or not, you're in love with Ellie Williams."

## Chapter Twelve

On Monday morning at work, Ellie stopped Cole in the hallway. "Hey, Cole, I think it does work better to go to the job sites in the morning. I'm glad you changed things," she said, flashing him a stunning smile.

Cole looked at her and muted a gulp. He had never seen Ellie look so agreeable and so—what was it—something about her eyes. They looked clear and sparkly; it was like looking into a lucid pool of water and seeing through to the bottom. Her face nearly glowed. He didn't know what, but something was clearly wrong. Maybe she needed a doctor. "Are you okay?" he asked.

"Yeah, I know. I'm surprised those words came from my mouth, too." She laughed, a laugh that said she enjoyed his company and wanted to spend more time together, he thought. He mentally shook his head. His brother's goofy talk had Cole all messed up.

She tipped her head to one side in a cute sort of way that brought a catch to his heart. "Maybe I'm changing," she said, her eyes encouraging him to linger. Uh-oh, he didn't like this.

"Yeah." He smiled in spite of himself. His jitters surprised him. He figured he must have had too much coffee at the coffee shop. Yeah, that was it. He needed to cut more of his caffeine. If Ellie noticed his discomfort, she didn't let on. She just stood there, smiling, twinkling, glowing. Using all the weapons that women use to snag a man.

He pulled at the collar of his shirt and loosened his tie. It was his habit to dress up for closings, though today, he wished he had ditched the tie. "Well, I'd better get going. I have an appointment."

"Okay," she said.

Their eyes locked. Another silent gulp. He had to get out of there. Something in her expression made him want to run as far and as fast as his legs could carry him. Don't panic, Cole, he told himself. Caed has you all worked up. Things are fine.

"Are you all right, Cole?" she asked. Concern shadowed her face while her hand reached up and touched his arm. His skin tingled in response, upsetting him all the more.

"I'm fine. See you later." Cole turned and practically ran down the hall.

No doubt about it, the woman was armed and dangerous.

Ellie smiled as she walked back to her desk. She hadn't seen Cole behave shyly before. The e-mails he had sent her definitely showed more confidence. She didn't mind. Their relationship was growing, and that's what mattered. She knew he had feelings for her, and now she knew how she felt about him.

Her world was changing, and as incredible as it seemed, she was all right with that.

By Friday morning, Cole woke up feeling as if he'd been run over. He'd wrestled all night with his bed covers and one glance at his bed told him they had won. Jerking off the remaining sheet, he thumped out of bed. He had to talk to Ellie today and get this whole mess cleared up.

Once showered, shaved and dressed, Cole walked into the kitchen where Caed sat eating cereal at the table. Caed looked up.

"Hey, Cole, I apologize for interfering with you and Ellie. You're right, I've been out of line. You want me to talk to her?"

Cole softened with his brother's apology. "No, I'm going to stop by her house after work. I thought it would be better than telling her at the office."

Caed nodded. "I could go with you since I don't leave until tomorrow afternoon, if you want."

Cole sighed. "Thanks, Caed, but rather than embarrass her further, I think it's best if I go alone."

"Okay. I promise it's my last attempt at matchmaking. You just don't cooperate."

Cole let out the smile he'd been holding back. "Well, that's one good thing from this whole situation."

The two brothers talked a little then Cole headed for work. Once he arrived at Wiley's Dream Homes, he stepped out of his car, noticing the slight nip in the air. He glanced around. Summer would be over before they knew it, with autumn right on its tail. Not that he minded so much. Autumn was his favorite time of the year, though he didn't care much for winter, other than for skiing.

"Good morning, Cole," Ellie said when he stepped into the office. His pulse surged with energy, as if he'd been running. He could almost feel the wind in his face, the blood charging through his veins. Something about her seemed so different these days.

He didn't like it one bit.

Mentally, he shook himself. She was out to hook him and that irritated him to no end. "Hi, Ellie," he said with his most professional voice.

His tone didn't seem to deter her in the least. "Are we going to the job sites together this morning?"

Oh, he had forgotten about that. Maybe that would be a good time to talk about their problem. He was feeling better already. The sooner he got this over with, the better.

"Yeah, that would be great. Will that work for you?" He looked at her incredulously. Right before his eyes, her face turned a soft crimson. Oh, she was good. Charm practically dripped from her. When he gulped, he could feel his Adam's apple stick halfway. He coughed and swallowed to get it moving again.

She lowered her eyelids ever so gently, allowing her thick lashes to brush lightly upon her cheek and then she looked up again. "That will work for me, Cole." Another smile.

He glanced at his palms. They were sweaty. His chest tightened and his breath hovered somewhere short of his lungs. He'd never had a panic attack before, but he wondered if he was experiencing one.

"Are you all right, Cole?" Ellie touched his arm. Again.

He coughed and struggled to breathe. "Fine," he barely managed, waving the matter away with his hand.

She smiled—or was it sneered? He couldn't tell for sure. She almost had a mocking look on her face. Yeah, that was it. No doubt she figured it was a matter of time before he would be wrapped around her little finger.

Suddenly, he saw himself in an apron with a smudge of flour on his face, pushing a broom. Another scene flashed through his mind showing Ellie lying on a couch while he fed her grapes. He swallowed hard to shake the images.

The last image took two swallows.

"Cole, what is it?" She looked concerned. Oh, sure, that's what she wanted him to think.

"I need a drink of water. I'll see you later." Before Ellie could respond, he was out of there. His heart still intact.

This time.

Ellie glanced at the clock. Time to meet Cole to go to the job sites. She took the last drink of her coffee. He sure seemed wound tight today. She wondered what was up. Lately, he had seemed uncomfortable around her. Everything she tried to do to put him at ease appeared to fail. He had to notice how she was trying to get along with him. She shrugged. No time to worry about it. Perhaps now that they had both admitted to their feelings he was a bit shy.

She liked that. Shy men were, well, endearing in a cute sort of way. With a smile on her face, she grabbed her notebook and purse, then headed for Cole's office. Yeah, she decided she liked the cute-little-boy look he put on when he felt shy. And to think at one time she'd seen him as a threat.

She couldn't imagine what she had been thinking.

"Hey, you ready to go?" she asked Cole when she slipped into his office.

He glanced up from his paperwork. "What? Oh, yeah." Jotting another note, he closed his file and grabbed a notebook. Together they left his room and walked out to his car.

By the time they had finished their work at the job sites, Cole noticed it was close to lunchtime. He got an idea. "Hey, since we're already out, you want to go to lunch?" he asked Ellie, hoping that would soften the blow of what he had to tell her.

She flashed him that smile again. "That would be great."

A moment of hesitation grabbed him. He wasn't sure he really wanted to do this, tell her the whole story. Once he told her what Caed had done, Cole might lose her forever. But then that was what he wanted, or so he told himself. Yet he couldn't deny his attraction to Ellie. He had even entertained the idea of dating her, really dating her, not just as friends, but the whole commitment thing bound him like a ball and chain. If it didn't work out, they'd be stuck working together, and that would be awkward for the both of them. No, better to stay friends and not let all that stuff get in the way.

Many times, he'd said he didn't plan on getting tied down with anyone, and that included Ellie Williams. Caed told him he repeated it over and over to convince himself.

Caed could be such a jerk sometimes.

Spotting an empty parking space, Cole pulled his SUV into it and killed the engine. He turned to Ellie and smiled. "You ready?"

She nodded and grabbed her purse. "Ready."

The fifties restaurant they entered had a checkerboard tile floor and red tables. Large posters of movie stars splashed across the walls in a colorful display. Hamburger and French-fry smells wafted through the room, while a jukebox crooned the oldies.

Once they slid into their booth, Cole mentally went over how he would tell Ellie. He wanted to say it in such a way that he would keep her friendship. No doubt her ego would get in the way, and she would feel embarrassed by it all. He had to admit he wanted to protect her from that. Cole didn't want to hurt her for anything, but somehow he felt there was no way around it.

After placing their orders, he leaned into

the table. Ellie glanced around the restaurant and then turned to look at Cole.

"I need to talk to you about something."

"Okay," she said with a smile and sat up taller in her seat as if she were about to hear good news.

Inward groan. He could wring Caed's neck for this. "Uh, I'm not sure how to approach it." He wanted to kick something, doggone it.

Ellie placed her hand on Cole's hand. "What is it, Cole?"

"Oh, no, no. I can't think when you do that." He pulled his hand away and placed it in his lap. Her face clearly registered that she didn't understand. Now he had her full attention.

"I guess you know that my brother is here visiting?"

She nodded. "I had heard that. I wondered when you were going to bring him into the office."

"Well now, there you see, that's just it." His hands slapped the table, and he leaned back against the booth.

Just then the waitress approached and began placing their food in front of them. Cole felt impatient with the interruption. When she finally left, he leaned back into the table to pick up where he had left off.

"Do you want to pray or do you want me to?" Ellie asked.

"Oh, uh, you can pray," he said, frustrated beyond belief.

Ellie whispered a prayer. Great. Now all of Heaven knew where they were and could watch him be a total jerk.

Could he help it if the thought of a lifetime commitment made him feel as if he was trapped in a room without oxygen?

One glance at the food on his plate made him sick.

"You know, Cole, you're looking a little pale."

Why, the woman was a genius. She should hang out her shingle and start practicing medicine.

"You need me to get you something?"

"Yeah, a hit man for my brother," he wanted to say. "No, I'll be fine."

"You were talking about your brother. You two have a problem or something?"

"Well, not exactly, um, it's kind of like this—" His cell phone rang. Cole shrugged and answered it.

"Have you explained things to Ellie yet?" Caed asked.

"Not yet."

"Oh, where are you?"

Cole glanced at Ellie who started to eat her lunch. "I'm at a restaurant—with Ellie."

Caed whistled. "Oh, sorry. I'm battin' a thousand, huh?"

"Something like that," Cole said, while watching Ellie with caution.

"I'll talk to you tonight. Sorry I interrupted."

"No problem, I'll get right on it."

"Oh, yeah, right. Okay, see ya, Cole."

"Bye." Cole snapped his phone closed.

"Everything okay?"

"Oh, yeah, just a subcontractor checking on something. I'll have to get back to him." Cole figured two interruptions were a sign from Heaven, so he decided to hold off telling Ellie at lunch. Some things just weren't meant to be—yet. "So, what are you doing this weekend?" With his fork, he dunked a couple of fries into a mound of catsup. Right after the words left his mouth, he regretted saying them. He looked up.

Ellie's face positively glowed. "Well, I'm planting a maple tree if you want to help," she teased.

He stared at her. "Why would you plant a maple tree? You already have trees in your yard."

"I know it sounds strange, but I've never been anywhere long enough to plant a tree and see it grow."

"People do that?" he asked. He could hear the horror in his voice.

"What?"

"Watch trees grow?" This woman definitely was not his type.

Ellie laughed. "Well, they don't actually sit and watch the tree grow, silly. It's just neat over time to realize how a tree is growing with you. Does that make sense?"

Cole took a bite and nodded, though it made no sense to him at all. Who cared if a tree grew while you were around? This woman needed a life.

"When I visit a few of my old friends, we talk about the trees in their yard, how they have grown over the years, remembering how small the trees were when we were kids, that kind of thing. It's kind of my way of putting down roots, pun aside."

Uh-oh, here it comes. He quickly took a drink of his iced tea. "Like you, I don't think I've been in one place longer than a couple of years, so other than seeing leaves in my yard come and go, I didn't really see much growth."

Ellie shrugged. "I admit it takes real commitment. You should try it sometime." She flashed him a winning grin.

Now he knew he was in trouble. *Roots. Commitment.* Just hearing those words made him break out in a cold sweat. He knew she kind of liked him, but he hadn't expected her to try and snare him so quickly. Cole glanced at his watch. "Oh, you know what? I have to get back. You ready to go?" He looked at her almost-empty plate.

"I'm ready," she said, sweetly. She didn't seem put out in the least that he'd had to cut the lunch short. No question about it, she had a plan. He had to think of something, and fast.

## Chapter Thirteen

"So, how did it go?" Caed wanted to know when Cole walked in the door that evening.

Cole stopped and glared at him.

"Uh-oh. Should I leave now?"

Cole walked over and dropped onto the couch. He rubbed his temples. "What am I going to do?"

"What happened?"

Cole stopped rubbing his head and looked at him. "Nothing happened, okay?"

"You didn't tell her?"

"No."

Caed groaned. "I got you into this mess. I'll get you out."

Cole was already shaking his head. "No way. I'll handle this myself. You've done enough already."

"I don't really understand what the problem is. So she thinks you sent her a couple of nice notes. What's the big deal?"

If he could have exhaled fire, this would have been a good time. "The big deal is, she's after me. And thanks to you, she thinks I'm after her."

Clasping his hands behind his head, Caed leaned back in his chair. "And that's a problem? I wish I had such problems." He whistled.

"Come on, Caed. This is serious. When she learns the truth, she'll be humiliated because not only will I know and she know, but you'll know."

Caed looked at him, puzzled.

"Don't you get it? The whole thing is an ego bruiser. I don't want to hurt her, but I'm sure not ready to walk down the aisle, either!" Cole raked his hand through his hair.

"I think if you leave it alone, it will die down. No more e-mails, she'll get the hint."

"I don't know," Cole said, feeling unconvinced.

"I'm telling you, she'll get over it. Just keep busy, and don't pay extra attention to her. She'll get the hint."

Cole was tired of thinking about it.

"Maybe you're right," he finally said. One thought nagged at him; did he really want her to get the hint?

"Trust me, I'm right," Caed said with authority, though Cole still didn't trust him.

Cole decided to push the matter aside. He stood to his feet. "You know, I'm starved," he said, already making his way to the kitchen.

"Hey, listen," Caed said, "I need to go to the store and pick up a few things for my trip. You want anything?"

Cole rummaged through the fridge. "No, thanks."

"Okay, I'll be back in a little while."

Rustling through the lettuce, cheese and lunch meat, Cole barely noticed when his brother went out the door.

Ellie had just put on her sweats to go for her evening walk when the doorbell rang. She'd already paid the paperboy, and her parents were out of town, so she couldn't imagine who would be at the door.

"Cole, hello," she said, wondering at the stern look on his face.

"Hi, Ellie. Okay if I come in?"

She nodded and stepped aside as he entered.

"I think we need to talk a minute, if you have the time." He searched her face for the answer.

She couldn't imagine what would be so urgent that he had to come by and talk to her instead of telling her at work. The look on his face suggested this wasn't a nice social call. He looked different somehow. She studied him. Something didn't seem quite right. Problems at a job site, no doubt. "Sure, Cole. Come in and sit down."

"Thanks." He settled onto the sofa. His face grew hard, expressionless.

"So, what's up?" she asked in a cheerful voice, hoping to lighten the tension a little.

"Um, I think we need to get something straight between us."

Ellie braced herself. She didn't like the sound of his voice, nor did she like the vibes he was sending her. Every nerve in her body set on edge; something was definitely wrong.

"We work together. We are friends. I like you, you like me. But, well, that's where it ends."

A pain shot through her, causing nausea to kick in. She gulped slightly, trying desperately to hold back the tears that threatened. She looked down and studied her hands. "Why are you telling me this, Cole?"

He looked at the carpet. "Um, I just didn't want anyone to get the wrong idea."

"You mean anyone like me?"

"Well, um, yeah."

"You mean because of all the e-mails and stuff?"

"Yes. I don't know what got into me. It was a phase or something. I don't know. But consider it a passing thing. I won't go there again."

"Oh, no problem," Ellie said, trying to blow it off. "To tell you the truth, I didn't give it much thought at all." Okay, so she fudged a bit. "I hope I didn't give you the impression—"

"No, no, you didn't. I just thought I should clear up any false ideas I might have given you."

She waved a hand. "Oh, my, no. I know how you are, always teasing."

He looked relieved.

She stood and walked him to the door. "Well, I appreciate you taking the time to clear the matter, though it really wasn't a problem." She smiled sweetly while wanting to rip off his toenails one by one.

Very slowly.

He looked surprised. "Well, I just wanted

to make it clear where we stood so it wouldn't interfere with our jobs."

"Oh, goodness, no," she said with a slight giggle. She opened the front door. "Thanks for stopping by." She flashed a smile, though the room around her began to spin in slow motion.

Her quick acceptance seemed to catch him off guard. He'd probably expected weeping, wailing and gnashing of teeth. What an egomaniac. She wanted to scream at him to get out. Instead, she trapped her tongue behind her teeth.

"Uh, okay. Thanks for understanding, Ellie."

She shrugged. "What's to understand? There was no misunderstanding in the first place, as far as I'm concerned."

"So we don't need to mention it again?"

"Exactly," she said, still smiling.

"See you at work," he said, then turned and walked outside.

"See ya." She waved, barely closing the door before a torrent of tears burst through her defenses and sent her running to her bedroom.

Cole heard the front door shove to a close, then some rustling of sacks in the kitchen. "Need help?" he called out.

"No, I think I've got it," Caed replied.

Cole listened a moment as his brother stuffed groceries in the fridge and cupboard. He was glad Caed had stayed with him, despite the mess of things he had made with Ellie.

"There, that ought to do it," Caed said with a smile. He flopped into the brown recliner and rubbed an apple on his pant leg.

"You didn't need to buy groceries, Caed."

"Hey, I've been eating your grub awhile, it's the least I could do."

"Thanks."

"No problem." Caed studied Cole a minute.

"What?"

"Oh, nothing, it's just that, well, I saw Ellie while I was out."

"Yeah?" Cole wondered if he should start worrying.

Caed put on his best face. "Yeah. I don't think you have anything to worry about. She thought I was you, and, well, she didn't seem all that interested."

Cole felt a slight ping, but ignored it. He lifted his chin a little. "How do you mean?"

"Oh, she was nice enough. She said hello, and we had some small talk, you know. But then she seemed in a hurry, and when I asked what she had to rush off to, she told me she had a date." Caed bit into his apple and chewed much longer than Cole wanted him to. "So, you see, I don't think you have anything to worry about at all."

Cole sat there a moment while Caed went after his apple with a vengeance. "Well, good," Cole said, though he wondered why he didn't feel so good.

Caed watched him.

"What?" Cole said, feeling agitated.

A smirk lifted on his face. "Oh, nothing," Caed said, finishing off his apple with renewed zest.

"I hate it when you do that," Cole snapped.

"Do what?"

"Say I told you so without saying it."

"What are you talking about?" Caed acted oblivious, licking the last scrap of apple from his fingers.

"I know what you're thinking."

Caed's eyebrows raised. "What?"

"You think I'm going to get jealous or something over Ellie dating. Well, I'm not in the least." Cole fumed, but tried not to show it.

"That's good," Caed said with the hint of a smile.

"Aw, you're pathetic," Cole said, waving his brother off. By the time he reached his bedroom, he realized he'd just proved his brother right.

Cole was jealous.

Ellie fell to her knees by her bedside. As the tears spilled, Ellie realized much more bothered her than just Cole's dismissal. She had a deeper problem. Way deeper. Cheryl was right. Ellie had a control issue. She wanted control of her life, wanted to run things her own way.

She pulled a tissue from the box on her nightstand. Slowly, the issues played in her mind. The unnecessary diets, the temper tantrums when things didn't go her way, the changes that sent her into a tizzy, they all added up to a control issue.

Not only that, but she would do anything to gain approval. No one can please everyone. She needed to learn to accept herself and strive to please the One who mattered most. God.

*"I hadn't seen it before now, Lord,"* she said through her tears. *"I didn't mean to take the control from You. I don't know when it happened. I've never been good with change,*

*but I didn't realize I'd started planning my life and taken the control from You.*"

More tears. Again, she wiped her face. *"Help me to please You and not worry about what others think. You've created me the way I am, help me to accept myself. I need You, Lord. Forgive me for leaving You out of my life."* She sat there awhile, just listening, worshipping.

By the time she got up, she felt lighter than she had in years, and that was without dieting. She smiled to herself. "I'm such a blockhead— Uh-oh, I forgot. I need to accept myself."

Thoughts of Cole coming to her house earlier surfaced, but she didn't feel the humiliation this time. She decided that belonged to the Lord, too, and she would leave the outcome to Him. All she had to concentrate on was her walk with Him and living life in general. She could handle that.

Now.

Though sorry to see his brother go, Cole was glad life could get back to normal. He wondered what Ellie would be like when he got to work this morning. Cole carefully eased the SUV out of the garage. Caed had assured him there was no problem with Ellie, and she was dating someone. He also suggested Cole not mention it, said she seemed to want to keep her personal life private.

Well, that was just fine with Cole. It didn't matter to him one way or the other what Ellie Williams did away from the office. He turned on his signal and pulled up to the traffic light. A thought hit him. "The flowers." He smacked the steering wheel with the heel of his palm. He remembered back to the day he had teased her about the flowers. She had acted really weird about it. Now it made sense. They weren't from his brother, after all. She must be seeing someone. It puzzled him as to why she didn't want him to know. He felt a stab to his pride. It's not like he cared if she dated someone.

Arriving at the office, he whipped into his parking place and shut off the engine. Maybe now that she was seeing someone, they could get down to business. The business of running Wiley's Dream Homes.

Ellie stood at the front desk talking with Alex when he entered. "Good morning," he said with a smile. They both greeted him cordially. He started to round the corner then turned back. "Oh, Ellie, I have to make a quick call to a subcontractor, so could you meet me in my office in about five minutes to go over the day's schedule?"

"Sure, Cole, no problem," she said, a little too cheerfully.

"Thanks." He turned and continued toward his office. He couldn't imagine why it irritated him that she was happy, and he certainly didn't want to investigate the matter. Better to push it aside and just forget it. Truth be told, he was afraid of what he might discover.

On the other hand, maybe he should try to get her to spill the truth about who she was dating and how things were going. After all, friends shared such things. And they were friends—at least he thought they were. It might make her feel more at ease, too, if the matter were aired. That's what he'd do.

She brought her files, writing paper and coffee into his office with a smile. "Hi," she said, her voice reminding him of a warm summer's day.

While she got settled in her seat, he glanced at her. She looked good today. Really good. The left side of her blond, silky hair was tucked behind her ear, revealing a dainty earring, while the other side sloped toward her chin. She looked, well, attractive.

Oh, great, he couldn't imagine what was coming over him. She always looked good, but today, there was something special about her.

"Okay, I'm finally ready," she said, poising her pen over the paper, awaiting his instructions.

"Oh, in a minute," he said, finding himself for once, surprisingly without a professional conversation-opener.

"Oh, do you want me to come back?" She started to rise.

"So, how are things?"

His question obviously puzzled her. "What do you mean?"

"Just in general," he said with casual indifference, denying to himself that he was snooping.

"Fine."

He waited, hoping for more, but she sat there, tight-lipped. This wouldn't be easy. Caed was right, she wanted to keep her personal life private.

She looked around the room as if she was bored.

He cleared his throat. She wasn't taking

the bait. He'd have to try the blunt approach. "Um, so how was your date?"

She jerked her head to him. "My what?"

"Your date," he repeated.

"I don't know what you're talking about."

He plodded further. "When I saw you at the store on Friday night, you said you had a date."

She looked at him as if he had a bug on his face. "Look, Cole, I don't know who you saw at the store Friday night, but it wasn't me."

"You weren't at the store?" He heard his voice shaking.

She shook her head. "After you left my house, I was home for the rest of the evening."

"After I left your house?" Her words slammed into him like a runaway locomotive.

"Are you all right? You do remember coming to my house, right? The little talk that we had?"

Cole wondered if he had just cause to murder his brother. He mentally shook his head; it probably wouldn't hold up in court. He couldn't stand it any longer. Walking over to his door, he closed it, and sat back down in his chair.

"Cole, what's wrong?"

He shook his head. "I have no idea how to say this, but it's only fair that you know the truth."

She held up her hand. "We've been through this, Cole. I know we're merely coworkers. There's nothing between us. We established that Friday night, remember? I told you I didn't think a thing about the e-mails."

He looked at her incredulously. "Okay, this has gone far enough."

She looked confused.

For the next few minutes, he told her the entire situation about Caed playing the part of Cole and how upset he had been by it, but didn't know how to fix it. He felt she had a right to know.

At first, she looked offended. Then she seemed to work through her pride, let the whole idea sink in, and finally, to Cole's eternal surprise, she laughed.

He couldn't believe it. His mouth practically gaped. "You're not mad?"

"Well, nobody likes to be made sport of, but I have to admit it is kind of funny. Boy, he sure looks like you."

Cole couldn't believe his ears. Never in a million years would he have expected such a response from her. "You're amazing."

She smiled. "Why is that?"

"Most women would be livid, but you, you laugh." He scratched his head.

She shrugged. "What can we do? It's over and done. He meant no harm. He had a little fun—"

"At our expense," he interjected.

"Okay, so at our expense. No one was hurt."

"You know, there's something different about you. You've changed somehow."

"You know, I really have." She told him the reason for her change, how she had finally given the control of her life to God, where it belonged.

Her words pricked his conscience. He knew he had some issues of his own, but he wasn't ready to deal with all that just yet.

They went through the day's agenda and got business out of the way. Ellie stood to leave.

"Ellie?"

"Yeah?"

"Change looks good on you."

"Thanks," she said with a smile that curled his toes.

Cole had the sneaking suspicion that his life was about to change.

But then, he could handle change, couldn't he?

# Chapter Fourteen

"How are you doing, Jax?" Ellie asked as she poured her morning coffee in the office kitchen. She put the pot down and really looked at him. Dark circles underlined his eyes, his hair looked a bit disheveled.

"Let's just say I've been better."

"What's wrong?" Ellie asked.

Jax put his finger to his mouth. He grabbed his mug of coffee and motioned for her to follow him. Once inside his office, he closed the door behind them. Ellie was a little worried. Jax normally wasn't so secretive. She waited while he settled into his chair and took a sip of coffee. He looked up. "I broke it off with Alex last night."

"Oh, Jax, I'm sorry."

He rubbed his jaw. "Alex is a nice woman, but well, she's just not the right one for me."

Ellie didn't know what to say to that. She took a drink of coffee. "Is she okay?"

"Well, we've been having some struggles lately, so I don't think she was all that surprised. She didn't say a whole lot, wished me well. I guess I should be happy about that, yet, something in her manner was a little unsettling to me." He looked toward his window as if thinking about it.

"What do you mean, Jax?"

He looked back to Ellie. "I don't know, exactly. It just didn't feel right, you know?"

Ellie nodded, but she wasn't at all sure she did know what he meant. "Do you think it will affect your working relationship?"

He grabbed a pencil between his fingers and started twirling it. "That's what I'm worried about," he said, watching the pencil.

"I'm sorry, Jax. I'll be praying for you both."

"Maybe she'll talk to you," he said, surprising Ellie.

"I—I don't know. Alex and I have never really been close friends."

He shrugged. "Well, if she does, put in a good word for me, okay?"

"To keep the peace?"

"Right."

"I'll see what I can do." She took another drink of coffee. "Everything else all right?"

"Yeah. Classes are going well. That was another problem, trying to keep her happy, get my work done here, and still work in class and homework time." He ran his hand through his hair. "I just couldn't do it all, and she didn't have the understanding to deal with it."

"Do you think there's a chance you could ever get back together?"

"No. It's just not there for me. I mean, Alex is a great woman and all, but we're just not a good fit."

Ellie nodded. "I'm sorry, Jax. You take care of yourself." She stood. "I'd better get back to work or my boss will get mad," she said with a wink.

"You mean me?" he teased.

"Well, you and, um, my other boss."

Jax raised his brows. "Oh, yeah, he is pretty ruthless."

She laughed and walked through the door. Frowning, Alex stood just outside the door, causing the smile to leave Ellie's face. Alex glared at her, then walked off in a huff.

Uh-oh, this might call for prayer and fast-ing, Ellie thought, making a hasty retreat to the safety of her desk.

Ellie reached up to knock on Cole's door but stopped short when she saw the worried look on his face. He glanced up just as she was about to leave.

"Ellie, you need something?"

She turned back to him. "Oh, it's nothing, Cole. It can wait."

"No, please, come on in." He motioned for her to sit in front of his desk.

She wished she hadn't come. The look on his face told her he wasn't in the mood for bad news. For a moment, she fell silent, staring at the floor.

"Ellie, what's wrong?"

She looked up. "Oh, uh—"

"Come on, Ellie. There's a problem. You've never been able to hide bad news." He let out a guarded smile.

She sighed deeply. "I'm sorry, Cole. I'm afraid there have been vandals at the Wilson job site."

His lips formed into a thin line. He blew out a long, deliberate breath and stared at his desk, slowly shaking his head. Ellie waited a moment, allowing the news to sink in.

"How bad?"

"Um, well, it's nothing a little paint won't cure," she said with her brightest voice. In a much softer tone she added, "We will have to rip out the carpet, though."

His face paled. "Graffiti?"

She nodded.

"How many rooms?"

"Um, actually, every room."

Cole slammed his fist on the desk. Ellie jumped. "Do the Wilsons know?"

"Not yet."

Cole stood and began to pace. "What is going on around here? Did they break into the house or was it unlocked?"

"I don't know the details. I just got the call this morning. I thought you might want to go over there with me and take a look."

"Where's Jax?"

"He had to go into school today to meet with his professor."

"Great. Just great." Ellie prayed a silent prayer, knowing the responsibility of all this weighed heavily upon Cole. "Okay, let's go," he said in a what-else-can-we-do tone.

"Well, it could have been worse," Cole said as he and Ellie pulled away from the job site in his car.

Ellie looked at him with obvious surprise.

He gave her a sideways glance. "What? You think I don't have a positive side?" He tossed her a weak smile.

She smiled warmly. "I confess it was a relief to see the carpet only had a spot or two in the back bedroom. That will be easy enough to replace. I had envisioned all the carpeting having to be replaced."

Cole nodded. "I am concerned about one thing, though."

"What's that?"

"How are these vandals getting into the house? There was no sign of forced entry, which means either they have a key or the door was left unlocked."

Ellie whirled her head around to look at him. "You think it's someone on the job?"

They pulled up to a stoplight and Cole turned to her. "Let's just hope not."

They drove the rest of the way back to the office in silence. Inside, Alex sat at the receptionist's desk wearing a bright smile. Cole noticed Ellie looked a little apprehensive when she spotted Alex. He wondered what that was all about.

"Hi, Cole," Alex said with unusual charm. "Could I talk to you a minute?"

He looked at Ellie.

"I'll talk to you later, Cole," Ellie said, leaving Alex and Cole alone in the front room.

"What's up?" he asked, when he reached Alex's desk.

She licked her lower lip. "Well, I need someone to talk to, and I know you're busy, but I wondered if you'd have lunch with me today?"

Cole couldn't have been more surprised by her request. "Where's Jax?" He didn't miss the shadow that crossed her face.

"He's at school today, as always." Her face brightened again. "So, will you go with me?"

Cole thought a moment. "Yeah, I think that would be fine. I don't have any appointments until three."

"Great." She perked up. She reached a hand up and touched his arm, unnerving him a little. "I'll look forward to it," she said with a tone that told him to run. Instead, he smiled weakly, and walked back to his office.

Puzzled by the whole affair, he wondered if he should talk to Ellie about it. But then the last time he had shared something with her, she had gone straight to Jax. No, he'd better wait and see what was up with Alex. Still, an uncomfortable feeling settled upon him, almost a feeling of doom. He couldn't quite figure it out.

Cole mentally shook his head. Those vandals had him suspicious of everything.

Ellie stopped at his door. "I'm getting a cup of coffee, and since you have been easing back into drinking the office coffee, I thought I'd ask if you want some."

Okay, now he really was getting suspicious. One woman invites him to lunch, another offers to get him coffee? Hmm, this was August. His birthday wasn't until October. Why the special treatment?

"Cole?" she asked with a heart-stopping smile.

Ellie's voice jarred him out of his musings. "Oh, sorry. Yeah, that would be great. Thanks, Ellie." He could hear her sandals clack on the hardwood floor as she walked down the hall. This was turning out to be a good day after all. He almost felt like leaning back in his chair and resting his feet on his desk. The phone on his desk rang, jarring him from a perfectly wonderful daydream.

"Hello," he said with a grouse.

"Well, hello to you, too," came Jax's voice. "Bad day?"

Cole wanted to say, "What would you know about it, you're never here," but he didn't. "Let's just say I've had better."

"Uh-oh. Listen, Cole, I'll be in this afternoon. If you want to schedule a time to meet, that would be great for me."

Cole rubbed his jaw. "Well, I'm going out to lunch with Ale—" He stopped himself, not sure how Jax would take the news.

"You're going to lunch with Alex?" Jax wanted to know.

"Yeah, do you mind?"

"Not at all."

"She said she needed to talk."

Jax whistled.

"What's that about?"

"You'll get an earful about me, no doubt."

Cole leaned into his chair and got comfortable. "What's going on with you two, you having a lovers' quarrel?" Cole smiled at Ellie as she brought him his coffee, and he mouthed "thank you." She threw him her heart-stopping smile once again, warming him clear through without benefit of the coffee. Ellie turned and walked out of his office, taking his thoughts with her.

"Cole, you still there?"

"Oh, yeah, sorry. Someone just came into my office. They're gone now."

"Well, as I was saying, we broke up."

Jax's words hit Cole with surprise. "You really did?" He thumped forward in his chair. "I figured when you told me you were having problems that you'd work things out." Feeling uncomfortable, Cole searched for something to say. "I'm sorry, Jax. If you need to talk, I'll be around."

"No need to feel sorry, it's just one of those things. It wasn't working, and well, I don't love her. We can talk more when I see you this afternoon. It's kind of complicated."

"Oh, great. I guess I will get an earful over lunch then. I'd better take some antacids with me."

Jax laughed. "If anyone can handle it, you can." A moment of silence stood between them. "Hey, listen, Cole, if you find yourself interested in Alex, it's not a problem for me."

"Oh, I don't see that happening," Cole assured him in a hurry.

"Well, just wanted you to know. I've gotta go. I'll see you, say, around two o'clock, will that work?"

"Sounds great. I checked my schedule. I

thought I had a three o'clock appointment, but it turns out it's not until four."

"Okay, I'll see you at two. Good luck at lunch."

"Thanks a lot." Cole placed the phone back in its cradle.

The next hour flew by while Cole pored over pressing paperwork.

"Hey, Mr. Workaholic, you ready for lunch?" Cole looked up to see Alex standing in his doorway. She was dressed in a white lace-trimmed tank, which he admired but which he wasn't at all sure was appropriate for an office setting. Her cream-colored pants hugged her legs, making her shape quite visible. Cole had a sneaking suspicion she'd planned it that way.

"I'm ready," he said, meaning it. After all, Jax said she was fair game. But, of course, he'd never really been interested in Alex. Still, she was nice to look at, and she would be a safe date. Her type didn't like commitment any more than he did. Yet, she had wanted to commit to Jax. He reluctantly followed her out of his office and out of the building.

She motioned him to her wine-colored luxury convertible. They climbed onto the leather seats. Cole whistled. "I think I have the wrong job."

Alex laughed. "Well, trust me, I didn't get this car on my income. A present from Daddy," she said, flashing a grin.

Cole raised an eyebrow. "Would he consider adopting a son?"

"Oh, that would never do," she said. "That would make you my brother, and well, we can't have that, can we?" Her eyes spoke volumes, and Cole felt his breath leave him as the ball and chain tightened around him again.

Alex put her key in the ignition and started the car.

"Do you mind?" he asked, reaching over to turn on the radio.

She shook her head. Just as they were pulling out of the lot, Ellie emerged from the building in time to see them. Cole waved, but the look on her face made him feel funny in a weird sort of way. Kind of like he had let her down or something. He shook his head. That's dumb. They didn't have an understanding between them, other than that they were mere friends.

"How about that new restaurant the staff went to a couple of weeks ago?" Alex asked, pulling into traffic.

"Sounds great."

They talked of the weather and office chitchat on the way to the restaurant. Ellie's expression haunted Cole all the way there.

Once seated in their booth and after placing their orders, Alex began. "I guess you know about me and Jax?" she asked, her eyes searching his face.

Cole wasn't at all sure he liked being placed in this situation. "I just found out."

"From whom?" she asked before taking a sip of her diet drink.

"Um, Jax called just before we left."

"Oh," she said with an obvious sneer in her voice. "And what did he tell you?"

"Look, Alex, I don't want to get in the middle of whatever is going on with you two."

She held up her hand. "You're totally right. I shouldn't have asked. Sorry."

Cole took a drink of his iced tea. "So why did you want to go to lunch with me?"

"Well, I noticed you and Ellie have kept your relationship purely professional from what I can see, and I thought maybe you and I could get together once in a while."

Oh, boy. He had been around bold, pushy women before, but this one should run for president. After all, Jax was his best friend, and he and Alex had just broken up. Cole wasn't at all sure he wanted to go there. "I don't know, Alex—"

"Look, Cole, I know you and Jax are great friends, but I don't think it's a problem."

"Are you trying to make him jealous?"

"Not at all. We had a good thing going for a while, but then it just didn't work out anymore. We have different interests. We're both ready to move on."

Cole stirred the ice in his glass. "Well, it takes time to get over relationships, Alex. I think you need to wait awhile."

"Who knows what I need better than I do?" she asked, sweetly, though Cole was sure her teeth were clenched.

"I'll have to think about it, Alex. In the meantime, let's just enjoy lunch."

She looked a little miffed, but said nothing further about it. They had a polite discussion over their entrées and returned to work unscathed. When they entered the building, Ellie stood in the foyer.

"Oh, hi, Ellie," Alex said, her voice thick with sweetness. She turned to Cole and placed her hand on his arm. "Thank you, Cole. I had a lovely time." She turned once more toward Ellie, flashed a smile, and walked over to her desk.

Cole watched the entire exchange with mouth gaping. He knew Alex meant to dig at Ellie, but he and Ellie didn't have anything going, so why would it matter? True, Ellie had given some indication of interest after that whole mess with Caed, but he wasn't sure about all that, either. She had fallen for Caed, after all, not him.

Ellie looked at him through sad eyes and offered a weak smile before turning back to her desk.

He gave an involuntary shudder. A sure sign of impending doom. He didn't like the feel of this. He didn't like it one bit.

# Chapter Fifteen

With the start of a new day, Cole poured himself a cup of coffee and glanced up just as Jax walked through the kitchen entrance. "Hey, guy, how ya doing?"

Jax gave a half smile. "I'll tell you after I drink some coffee."

Cole grinned and pulled a mug from the cabinet. He filled a cup for Jax and handed it to him. Cole let him in on the latest happenings at the construction sites and they talked of the business in general. While they were talking, Alex came into the room.

"Hello, Jax," she said with a cool edge to her voice. She looked to Cole and managed a huge smile. "Cole, how are you?" She laid her hand on his arm and let it linger there, making him uncomfortable. He wished she'd quit doing that.

"I'm fine, Alex," he answered, stepping free from her touch. If she noticed his obvious attempt to get away from her, she didn't let on. She seemed more intent on watching Jax.

Taking her time, she poured herself a cup of coffee, added sugar and cream, then turned to the guys. "You don't have to stop talking on my account," she said sweetly. She stopped and took a drink of her coffee, then walked toward the door. Cole and Jax watched her, saying nothing. She turned around once again. "Oh, Cole, would you call me tonight? I need to talk to you about something." Her eyes pinned him as she waited for his answer.

"Uh, sure," he said, feeling put on the spot. Just then he noticed Ellie standing to the side of the entrance. Her face registered surprise. No doubt she had heard Alex's comments. Alex strutted from the room with all the arrogance of a peacock.

"Morning, Jax. Cole." Ellie helped herself to the coffee.

Jax and Ellie engaged in some light conversation while Cole watched her. She wouldn't look at him, though her cheeks turned a slight crimson. The color of her pantsuit heightened the green of her eyes, making her look incredible. He tried to turn away, but he just couldn't stop looking at her. Ever since she'd made her commitment, as she called it, to the Lord, she had a definite glow about her.

He had always thought it bogus when people said Christians had a glow about them. Now, looking at Ellie, he believed it was true. Since meeting with Jax and studying the book of John, he had learned a lot. Still, something held him back from making a real commitment.

Okay, so he had a problem with commitments. But God could make a person overcome anything, right?

"Cole, are you okay?" Jax nudged him.

Cole's eyes refocused and he saw Ellie and Jax staring at him. "Oh, sorry, guess I got caught daydreaming."

Ellie smiled. "Happens to the best of us."

Cole remembered the meeting where he had pulled her out of a daydream and embarrassed her in front of the staff. "I guess it does at that," he said with a definite tone of apology. Jax and Ellie continued to look at him. Feeling a mite uncomfortable, Cole decided this was a good time to flee. "Well, I'd better get to work," he said, already edging his way through the kitchen.

Back in his office, Cole shut his door. For some reason, he felt the need to be alone. Alex was getting on his nerves, constantly putting him in the middle of her breakup with Jax. Ellie herself had become a constant source of contradictions. One minute she played Miss Professional, the next, she betrayed him with a smile that made his insides turn squishy. He'd said it before, and he would say it again, the woman was dangerous.

He opened a drawer to pull out a file and noticed the Bible Jax had left for him in the office. No one could see into his office, so Cole decided to pick it up and just stroll through it for a moment. Scripture after Scripture spoke to his heart. He wanted to make a change, and needed to make a change in his life, but how could he be sure he could trust this God of the Bible? He had trusted his mom, and she had deserted their family. He had trusted his dad who drank himself to an early grave. But his grandmother, well, he couldn't deny her obvious walk with the

Lord. She had that glow about her, too. If anyone could make him believe, it was her. His heart grew soft. How long he sat there lost in the memories, he wasn't sure. He finally picked up his phone and punched Jax's intercom number.

"Hello?"

"Hey, Jax, are you free tonight or do you have class?"

"I'm free. What do you have in mind?"

"Um, I thought maybe we could go to dinner and discuss some things."

"Don't forget you have an important phone call to make," Jax teased.

"Huh? Oh, you mean Alex?"

"That's the one."

"I'm not too worried about that."

Jax laughed. "I'm sorry to get you in the middle of all this, Cole."

"You're not the one who is putting me there. Besides, I need to deal with it."

"Actually, if she makes things too uncomfortable, I'll have to deal with it," Jax said, with a tinge of worry in his voice. "I thought we could still work together, but now I'm beginning to wonder."

"Well, give it some time. Maybe things will all work out after a little while."

"Maybe." Jax didn't sound convinced. "So, when do you want to meet and where?"

"How about Grant's Steakhouse at six-thirty?"

"I'll see you there."

"Great." Cole hung up the phone. He didn't know where the evening would take him, but he decided it was worth checking out.

Ellie and Cheryl settled into a corner booth at Grant's Steakhouse. The waitress took their drink orders and passed out the menus. The hum of conversation around them and the heady scent of barbecue began to soothe Ellie.

She glanced at the menu and rolled her head from side to side.

"Tense day?" Cheryl asked.

Ellie sighed. "Yeah, a little."

Cheryl folded her menu and laid it down. "So, what's up?"

"Did you already pick your meal?"

"Yeah. I always get their Cobb salad. It's the best."

"I should do that, too…"

"Because you want it or because you're on a diet?"

Ellie smiled. "You'll be happy to know I haven't dieted for two weeks now." She frowned. "Which reminds me, I have tons of tomato juice, cabbage and diet meal shakes to get rid of."

Cheryl laughed. "I must say, I'm impressed."

Ellie told Cheryl how she had surrendered her "control" problem to the Lord.

"That's great, Ellie. Finally, I can relax and not feel guilty that I'm not dieting when you are. After all, I need to lose ten pounds, you don't."

Ellie laughed. "You look great the way you are. Aren't we women so silly?" Ellie glanced around the room. "Oh, no, look who just walked in."

Cheryl followed Ellie's gaze. Cole and Jax stood talking to the hostess at the front of the restaurant. "Is that a problem?"

Ellie slouched down in her seat and cupped her hand over her eyes as if that could stop them from seeing her. "No, but I just hope they don't spot us and try to sit with us. I wanted to talk to you alone tonight."

"Look, she's taking them to the other side of the restaurant."

Ellie glanced up. "Oh, good."

The waitress served them their drinks.

"So how is business going?" Cheryl asked.

Ellie shared some of her latest business dealings. "You know, things are strange with Alex and Cole right now. I think they might be dating."

Cheryl had taken a sip of her pop and almost choked. She coughed a few times, gasped, and finally managed a "You're kidding!" One more drink. "Did she and Jax break up?"

"You mean I didn't tell you?"

Cheryl shook her head furiously.

"Yep. Jax broke up with her the other day. Now she's hovering over Cole."

Cheryl stirred the ice around in her glass. "Do you think she's trying to make Jax jealous, or do you think she really likes Cole?"

Ellie thought a moment. "I'm not sure. I just hope she doesn't break up their friendship."

"Why would she? After all, Jax dumped her."

"Yeah, but you know how guys are, they always want what they can't have."

Cheryl shrugged. "I suppose that's true." She stirred her ice some more. "So how about you, how do you feel about the idea of her and Cole dating?" She stopped twirling the ice and looked up.

"What's it to me? If they want to date, that's their business." Though she said the words with boldness, they rang as hollow in the air as they did in her heart.

"You didn't answer my question. How do you feel about it?"

"I don't know."

"Ellie?"

"Look, Cole is a coworker, nothing more. He made it clear that's all he wants to be."

"You said he told you that it was his brother, Caed, who had said all that."

"True, but it's not like Cole said he wanted it to be any different. Besides, we're total opposites."

"In what way?"

"Number one, he doesn't share my faith. Number two, our personalities don't mesh. It would never work."

"Opposites attract, you know."

The waitress stopped at their table and placed food in front of them. Once she left, Cheryl said the prayer over their meal and they picked up their forks.

"I see what you mean about the faith thing, though. That's important."

"Exactly," Ellie said before scooping a bite of potatoes onto her fork and into her mouth.

They passed the rest of their meal with friendly chitchat, catching up on each other's lives. Ellie couldn't help glancing over at Cole and Jax from time to time. Though they were partially hidden from her view, if she leaned back just right, she could see them. Cole's expression appeared quite serious all through the meal, as if something troubled him. A thought struck her. Maybe he was telling Jax he wanted to leave the business. Jax had said many times he didn't know how long Cole would stay. That's why it had been so hard for Ellie to understand why Jax had made Cole a partner.

"Are you okay?" Cheryl wanted to know.

"Yeah, fine."

Cheryl followed her gaze. "Oh, you can see the guys from there?" She raised her eyebrows with suspicion.

Ellie felt her cheeks grow warm. "Okay, guilty as charged."

"You see, you do care about him."

Ellie could feel her eye twitch, just the way Cole said it did when she was nervous. When had it started doing that? She couldn't remember that happening before Cole had entered her life. "Cole looks serious. Makes me wonder if he's going to quit or something."

Cheryl looked surprised. "Why would you say that? Has he given any indication that he would?"

Ellie touched her eye to make it stop twitching. Fortunately, the lighting was subdued, so she hoped Cheryl wouldn't notice. "No, not really. But Jax has told me Cole is hard to pin down. He doesn't like commitments."

"Do you think he's running from Alex?"

Ellie looked at her. "I hope not. I would hate to think that Alex is chasing him off."

"It will be interesting to see how this all shakes out," Cheryl said, taking the last bite of her green beans.

They talked a little while longer. Ellie dared another glance at Cole's table. It looked as though their heads were bowed. That puzzled her. They couldn't be praying. Must be studying some paperwork, she decided.

Cheryl put her napkin on her plate. "You ready to go?"

"Sure."

They placed their money in the plastic

folder for the waitress and headed out of the restaurant. Once outside, Ellie fished through her purse for her keys. "Oh, good grief, I laid my keys on the table when I got my money out. I have to go back inside."

"Want me to wait?"

"No, that's okay. I'll talk to you later. Thanks for meeting me for dinner."

"My pleasure, girlfriend. See you soon."

The two friends hugged and Ellie headed back inside. She walked hurriedly over to the table. The waitress held Ellie's keys in her hand. "Excuse me, those are my keys. I just left them behind."

The waitress smiled. "Oh, good. I wondered if they belonged to you or the other lady, and I wondered how I was going to get them to you." She handed the keys to Ellie.

"Thanks a lot. I would have been in trouble without them," Ellie said, turning to go. At the front entrance, Cole stepped up behind her.

"Well, hello."

She recognized his voice instantly. "Hi." She looked around. "Where's Jax?"

"He already left. Had to meet with a professor. I waited and paid the bill. Nice guy."

She smiled as they pushed through the doors and stepped into the evening air.

"I can't help feeling I need to top off my meal with an espresso. Want to join me?"

His question caught her off guard.

"I still don't bite." His eyes twinkled with mischief.

"I think you've mentioned that a few times."

"And?"

"And what?"

"Have I bitten you yet?"

Ellie pretended to think awhile about that.

He raised his eyebrows. "Come on, Ellie, trust me."

There was a bit of a plea in his statement. Something about the way he said it caused the strains of "Kumbayah" to stir again. Why couldn't she get that stupid song out of her mind? She knew she had gone to one too many camps.

"Well?"

The tune came to the forefront. She wanted to sway, start humming, and pull out a bag of marshmallows. Instead, she simply said, "I'd like that."

"Great. You can ride with me, or I can meet you at Tasty Grounds, which do you prefer?"

"How about I meet you there?"

He looked at her, a smile in his eyes. "One of these days you'll trust me. I can feel it."

His words wrapped around her in a snug fit. Funny, this was one time she didn't mind things fitting snugly. She smiled and walked toward her car. She was actually meeting Cole Preston for coffee.

Was this a date?

## Chapter Sixteen

Ellie got out of her car and looked up at the full moon which hung suspended over a distant maple tree. The air held a pleasant breeze, with no hint of the muggy weather they had experienced the week before. She pulled the strap of her purse over her shoulder and waited a moment for Cole to get out of his car. They walked toward the door of the coffee shop together.

"Boy, it's a nice evening," Cole said, opening the door for Ellie.

She felt warm but shivered in spite of herself. Something about this man did that to her. She just hoped her eye wouldn't twitch.

Once inside, the rich smells of coffee assailed her. Talk about a comfort food—mochas certainly did the trick for her. The whirring of the espresso machine and the contented chatter of patrons made her glad to be there. Especially with Cole.

Looking around, Ellie found an empty wooden table for them while Cole ordered her mocha and his espresso. She settled into a seat, pulled out a mirror and checked her makeup, then put it away just as Cole turned to walk toward the table.

"One skinny mocha with whipped cream," he said, handing the hot drink to her.

"Thank you, Cole."

"Hopefully, we won't stir up a tornado this time," he said, tossing her a wink.

She grimaced. "Don't remind me."

"Hey, it wasn't all that bad. We got free drinks, after all."

"True," Ellie said with a chuckle. "Wonder if Amy is working tonight." She glanced over at the counter.

Cole looked, too. He shook his head. "I didn't see her when I was over there."

"That was a trip to the coffee shop I won't soon forget."

Cole laughed. "Me, either." He stretched his long legs to the side. "Boy, I need to start running again. My legs have been aching lately."

"It does help to stretch them out. I don't run, but I do walk a lot at the park near my house."

He nodded and took a drink of his coffee. "I've been there. Nice park. In fact, that's usually where I go to run when I have the time."

"Really?" Ellie commented with a smile. "I'm surprised I haven't seen you there since I'm over there a lot."

"Like I said, I need to start up again. Unfortunately, it's been a while."

Ellie smiled and gave an understanding nod.

"So I guess you're wondering why I asked you to come here?" Cole asked, putting down his cup.

Uh-oh, she hoped this wasn't another let's-just-be-friends speech. Wait a minute, that was Caed. "I thought you were just being a good friend," she said cheerfully.

"Well, truthfully, I did just want to spend some time together. With all that's happened since Caed whisked into town, well, let's just say we've had one thing after another, and I'd like to start over—again."

Ellie laughed. "We do that a lot."

"Yeah. Lots of beginnings, never an ending?"

The look on his face told Ellie he had surprised himself in saying that. She smiled but said nothing.

"Actually…" He toyed with the jacket on his coffee cup. "I know you're a woman of faith. You've told me so yourself."

His comment surprised her. She looked at him with caution, hoping she hadn't done anything to offend him.

"I've been doing a little searching of my own."

Now he really had her interest piqued.

"Jax and I have been meeting weekly to study the book of John for some time now, and, um, well, tonight, I took a huge step. I prayed a prayer of commitment to the Lord."

Ellie stared at him, speechless.

He looked a little sheepish. "Hard to believe a guy like me could do that?"

She blinked. "Oh, no, not at all, Cole." Without thinking, she reached over and cupped his hand in her own. "I think it's wonderful." Tears filled her eyes.

"Now, don't get sappy on me. You might make me cry." He laughed.

She giggled and reached into her purse for a tissue.

"I've been wanting to do it for some time

now, but just didn't know how or if I could take the step. This is a whole new world for me. Commitment. Letting go of things and trusting Him. But I've been learning a lot from my study and also from going to your church. Listening to your pastor has made me want to know more."

"Cole, that's great. I'm so happy for you."

"Thanks." For a moment, they both drank from their cups, lost in thought.

"You know, Ellie, another reason I wanted to talk to you was, well, I want to be friends. I don't want us to feel all weird around each other anymore, you know what I mean?"

She smiled and nodded.

"I'm not saying you have to marry me, but I could always use a friend."

Ellie laughed a little, though she wasn't sure how to take his comment. She couldn't deny that she wanted to be more than friends and had felt a twinge of disappointment, but Cole seemed to want her friendship most of all. God is in control, she told herself. If Cole wanted friendship, that's what she would give him. If they had no future together, so be it. But she would be there to answer his questions about God and help him as much as she could.

They talked together awhile, long past

the time the last drop of their coffee had been drained from the cups. Ellie glanced at her watch.

"Uh-oh, I've kept you out too late. Your dad will have my hide."

Ellie laughed. "Not my dad, but my boss might if I'm too tired to show up for work in the morning."

"Oh, boy, we can't have that," he teased. "You ready to go?"

She nodded.

They picked up their paper cups, tossed them into a trash dispenser, then walked outside together. "Hey, thanks for meeting me, Ellie. You're a good friend."

Okay, she got the idea already. If he said that word one more time, she might have to hurt him. "You're welcome, Cole," she answered, pleasantly. She turned toward her car and headed for home.

The next morning, Alex and Cole stood huddled in a corner of the kitchen whispering about something when Ellie walked into the room for a glass of water. She had a headache. Alex looked up and then back to Cole, ignoring Ellie altogether. Cole turned his back toward Alex and looked at Ellie.

"Morning, Ellie," he said, with his dazzling smile.

"Hi, Cole. Alex," Ellie said. Alex barely gave a noticeable nod. Her face looked pinched, as if she was in pain. By the looks of her tight pants, Ellie figured the circulation to her legs had stopped. That was bound to cause discomfort. Just the very idea made her feel better, though she tried to feel sufficiently ashamed of herself.

"Will you meet me in my office when you're done in here, Ellie? We need to go over the schedule."

"Sure."

Ellie didn't miss the look that flickered on Alex's face. No question about it, Alex was after Cole, and she didn't want Ellie to get in the way. Ellie couldn't help but wonder, though, if Alex really liked Cole or if she wanted to make Jax jealous. Oh, well. Ellie didn't have time to think about it. She had a headache to get over and then work to do.

By the end of the day, her headache had finally subsided and Ellie could hardly wait to get home. She planned to eat a sandwich at home. Then she'd grab her light yellow sheet, since it was too hot to lie on a blanket, and her latest suspense novel before heading over to the park. The evening was perfect, and she wanted to spend it outside in the fresh air.

By the time she had pulled on her beige shorts, a cream T-shirt and brown sandals, and had twisted her hair into a clip at the back of her head, it was almost seven o'clock. She didn't mind, though. The park stayed pretty active with people this time of year until about nine or ten.

She parked her car and spotted a nice grassy knoll. Walking over, she spread her sheet out and settled down with her book. Murmurs sounded around her as people walked on a nearby path. What a perfect spot. She could stay here forever. Feeling a wave of contentment, she opened her book and started reading the first paragraph of the sixth chapter.

"Well, you just never know who you'll run into." Cole's voice sounded behind her.

Ellie turned around to see Cole silhouetted against the backdrop of a fiery setting sun. "Hi, Cole."

"Okay if I sit for a minute?"

"Sure," she said, pointing to a spot on the sheet. She put her book down, but somehow wasn't disappointed by the interruption. As he settled into place, she couldn't help but watch him. A navy T-shirt hugged his muscular chest, and khaki shorts stopped just above his knees. White crew socks and sturdy athletic shoes completed his runner's outfit. His arms glistened in the sunlight but he didn't look sweaty, just active.

"Been running?"

"Not too long. Just started a half mile back, really. I thought I'd stop and say hi, though."

"I'm glad you did," she said, meaning it.

Cole stared at her a moment. She felt a little awkward and glanced down. A slight breeze stirred between them. When she glanced back up, a ruffle of wind had lifted Cole's hair a smidgen until it peaked like the crown of an agitated bird. Ellie stifled a laugh with her hand.

"What?" he asked.

She dared to look up again. That was her mistake. For the life of her, she couldn't hold it in. Giggles poured from her until she finally gave way to a full-fledged guffaw. Tears streamed down her face and her stomach ached from laughing. Being a good sport, Cole laughed with her, though he did manage to smooth down his polly-want-a-cracker do.

After they both calmed down from laughing, Ellie apologized. "I don't know why that struck me so funny, but I think I needed a good laugh like that." She looked at him sheepishly. "Sorry it was at your expense."

"Oh, you'll get yours, Miss Williams," he said with an ornery grin. "Besides, I like hearing you laugh. I don't think I've ever heard you laugh before."

"Isn't that awful? I think I take life too seriously."

He kept watching her. "What would you think about, um, I mean, what would you say…"

She watched him, waiting for him to spit the words out. He was obviously struggling.

"Oh, now I'm acting like a tongue-tied kid."

She grinned.

"Now, don't you start laughing again," he said, shaking a finger at her.

"Wasn't going to," she said, with the Scout's honor sign.

"What would you say to going out once in a while?" He waited a second and then quickly added, "I mean, as friends, you know."

Her face grew warm. She felt light as a feather. "I'd like that," she said, deciding whatever the future held for them didn't matter. She would simply enjoy being friends with this man.

"Great," he said, flashing his trademark smile. Boy, she'd like to market those pearly whites. "Well, I'd better get back to running and let you get back to your book."

"Thanks for stopping by."

"My pleasure." He looked as though he meant it.

She watched as he ran away, literally. It was all she could do not to run after him....

The week went well. Ellie's estimation of Cole went up with every passing day. Perhaps they had crossed the hurdle of their differences and were on the other side of their friendship. She liked this side.

The phone on her desk rang and Ellie jumped. "Hello?"

"Ellie, could you come into my office?" Cole asked.

"Sure. I'll be right there." She hung up the phone and grabbed a notepad and pen. Hurrying to his office, she knocked at his door and he motioned her to come in. Jax stood by the window, watching her. The look on his face told her this couldn't be good. "So, what's up," she asked, trying to stay positive, as she settled into the chair across from his desk.

"Well, the strangest thing. You know the carpet we talked about for the Gibsons' home?"

"Yeah. I'm sorry about that. I meant to get that ordered last week, but didn't get to it. I can order it as soon as I leave here. I didn't know the painters were finished." She glanced at Jax whose face stayed expressionless. Goodness, what had she done?

"You didn't order it already?"

She looked at him, puzzled. "No. I was swamped with paperwork, and didn't get that far down on my to-do list. Why, is there a problem?" They still had plenty of time to get the carpet ordered as far as she knew. Why the third degree?

"How strange." He rubbed his jaw.

"Cole, Jax, what is it?"

"Well, first of all, the carpet was ordered and it was delivered by E-Z Carpets."

"What? We never do business with them."

"Exactly." He stared at her, as if the answer to the puzzle was on her face. "And they said it was ordered by Ellie Williams."

Ellie was taken aback. "Well, that's crazy.

I never order from them. Why would they say that?"

"That's a very good question."

"Can't we just send it back?"

"Unfortunately, the carpet guys went out there and already installed carpet in two of the rooms. The good news is one of our crew was there, noticed it was from E-Z Carpets, and knew we didn't do business with them. That's when he called me."

"Oh, Cole, I'm so sorry."

"I'm just wondering how it happened." He sat thinking, then finally shrugged. "Oh, well, there's nothing we can do about it. It was a phone order, and we have no way of proving we didn't order it. They even had our account number. We'll save the extra carpet and see if we can use it for something else."

"Again, I'm sorry."

"You're sure you didn't accidentally call them?"

"Quite sure. How could I accidentally call them?"

"Well, you might have copied the wrong phone number down."

"I would know if I had called someone and ordered carpet. I didn't call them."

"You're sure?"

"Look, Cole, I said I didn't call them."

"Okay. Thanks."

Feeling dismissed, Ellie stood and walked out of the room, but not before catching a doubtful glance between Cole and Jax.

Discouraged, Ellie walked back to her desk and tried to sort through the mystery. Was there any possibility she could have called the carpet company and just forgotten? But if that were true, she would have called their regular company, she wouldn't have called E-Z Carpets. Everyone in town knew they sold inferior carpet. Someone from another company could have ordered it, but why would they leave Ellie's name? Even if there was another Ellie Williams, that didn't explain using Wiley's Dream Homes' credit card number. None of it made any sense.

To make matters worse, Jax and Cole didn't believe her. She could tell by their expressions. They probably thought she had messed up and didn't want to admit to it. She wanted to prove her innocence but had no idea how to do it.

Somehow, Ellie had managed to get through the day. Feeling an injustice had been done but finding no way to absolve herself of the accusations left her feeling heavy-hearted. What hurt most of all was knowing that Jax and Cole doubted her integrity. After all this time, she would have thought they would know her better. Obviously, she was wrong.

No one bothered to come and talk to her any more about the matter in the afternoon. Work continued as if nothing had happened. She could almost see Jax in a long, flowing judge's robe, gavel in hand, and Cole sitting in the witness stand, pointing at her, his dark eyes flashing with judgment, charging "Guilty! She is guilty!"

Condemned without a fair trial.

Okay, so maybe she was overreacting. She just wanted to go home where life was safe and chocolate was in abundance.

## Chapter Seventeen

Cole shoved the paperwork from his desk into a file and decided to call it a day. He felt tired. Bone-tired. He couldn't imagine what the mix-up had been with the carpet, but maybe he had come down a little too hard on Ellie. He found it hard to believe she could have messed up like that. Still, he had no clue what had really happened.

He stood and stretched. Not much he could do about it now. Maybe he'd grab a sandwich and stop by Ellie's on the way home, make sure she was all right.

By the time Cole pulled into Ellie's driveway, dusk had settled upon the quiet neighborhood. A light from the living room spilled onto her lawn. Good, she was home. Cole walked up to her door, pushed the button and waited for her to answer.

"Hi, Cole," Ellie said with surprise when she opened the door. Her hair was disheveled, dirt smudged her face and jeans, and she held garden gloves in her hands.

"Um, may I come in or is this a bad time?"

"Oh, no problem," she said, stepping aside. "I just finished planting my tree. Have a seat."

He walked over to the sofa and sat down. "So you got your tree planted?"

"Uh-huh." A pleasant smile lit her face.

He couldn't help noticing how the smudges gave her the appearance of childlike innocence. She pushed a stray hair from her face, leaving another smudge behind on her forehead. He smiled.

"Oh, I'm forgetting myself. Would you like some tea?"

"That would be great," he answered, getting up and following her into the kitchen. "Let me help." Seeing Ellie wash her hands with the hand soap at the sink, Cole decided to follow suit. His hands felt sticky after having eaten French fries at dinner. "Okay if I wash my hands?"

"Sure, help yourself," she said, dropping ice cubes in glasses.

Cole looked through the kitchen window as he washed his hands. "Hey, your tree looks nice." Okay, so he exaggerated. The tree was only about two feet tall and was the scraggliest-looking thing he had ever seen. Reminded him of Charlie Brown's Christmas tree.

Ellie looked as proud as if she'd just given birth to a seven-pound baby boy. "Yep, that's my maple. I told you I was going to plant one."

Cole looked back at her and smiled. "Roots."

"Roots," she said, simply. Yet the word seemed to hold much more meaning than either was saying.

"So, you're committed to this tree now, you know. You won't be able to just up and move. You're stuck."

Ellie looked positively glowing. "I know. It's wonderful to belong." She handed him his iced tea and they walked back into the living room.

"I don't think I've stayed in one place long enough for flowers to bloom, let alone trees," Cole said, taking a drink of his tea.

Ellie laughed. "You should try it sometime. It's not such a bad thing to have roots."

Uh-oh, he didn't want to get into that. He cleared his throat and drank some more tea. "Look, I just wanted to apologize for what happened today. I didn't want you to think you were being called on the carpet, um, so to speak."

She looked up and made a face.

He groaned. "Okay, so that was bad," he said with a chuckle. "Seriously, we're just trying to get to the bottom of what happened."

"I understand," she said in a way that made him wonder if she truly understood at all.

"It's a hard one to figure out, but, well, what's done is done."

"Honestly, Cole, I have no clue what happened. I'd like to get to the bottom of it myself. I don't like it that they used my name, and I don't like it that someone has our credit card number."

"Well, they don't anymore. I canceled it."

"Good idea," she agreed.

Silence stretched between them, while they enjoyed their tea. "Well, I shouldn't keep you," he said, though he didn't rise. "I just wanted to make sure you knew we weren't blaming you." He finished the remainder of his tea.

"You think I'm still pouting over you getting the partnership?" she asked with a tease in her voice.

"A guy can't be too careful." He laughed it off, though he had to admit the fact she even brought the partnership thing up surprised him. The mere mention of it made him think it must still be on her mind. He had thought they were way past that.

They talked awhile longer. Then Cole finally stood. "Well, Ellie, I thank you for your hospitality, but I've kept you long enough. I'll just put this in the kitchen." He headed for the kitchen before she could protest. She followed him and placed her glass in the sink right behind him.

He turned suddenly, his face inches from hers. She looked up at him. Smudges and all, she looked...inviting. Before either of them could blink, his arms wrapped around her and his lips claimed hers. He pulled her tighter against him, each lost in the sweetness of the kiss, lost in one another, as if they had been waiting for this moment. His hands worked through her hair, his skin tingling at the silkiness of it. The heady scent of her perfume filled his senses. He lingered in her fragrance, the softness of her skin, the sound and feel of her breath upon his face. When at last Ellie pulled away, he was dazed. And angry.

With himself.

They stood in an awkward silence, still inches apart, both breathless. "I'm sorry, Ellie. I don't know what came over me."

She looked up at him. Still desirable, still too close for him to think straight. He had to get out of there—and fast. He took two steps sideways. "I'll—I'll see you tomorrow," he stammered, heading to the door as if to a getaway car.

"Okay," she said quietly.

Practically jogging to keep up with him, she followed him to the door and watched him with those big, green eyes. Eyes that seemed to say—no, he couldn't think about it. "Bye, Ellie," he said, not daring to look back.

"Bye."

He heard her door close behind him and only then took a breath, thankful he couldn't see her anymore. Once inside his car, he started the engine and backed out of the driveway. When he pulled onto the road, he finally felt safe. The thought struck him that it was funny that he would feel unsafe around that little wisp of a thing. "Ellie Williams." Just saying her name felt good on his tongue. It wasn't only the kiss, though he couldn't deny a definite physical attraction between them. Still, he knew things had been happening in his heart toward her. And he wasn't sure he was ready for it.

Commitment. Roots. The tree. Those thoughts continued to chill him to the bone. Yet, when he said Ellie's name, a shiver of another kind ran through him.

"Ellie, what are you doing here?" her mother wanted to know when she opened the door.

"Well, you are, after all, my parents. Can't I come by for a visit?" Ellie stepped into the house.

"Of course, dear, but it's eight-thirty. You don't usually stop in this late. Everything all right?"

"Yeah, I was just bored and thought I'd see what you two were doing."

Her mother laughed. "Well, come on in and have some tea with me. Your father is at a worship committee meeting."

Ellie's eye started twitching. Good grief. She didn't think a person could develop tics later in life. Thanks a lot, Cole, she thought with a bit of malice. Then the memory of the kiss played across her mind. She absently touched her lips.

"Are you all right, Ellie, you look a little flushed," her mother asked with a worrisome edge to her voice.

Ellie practically gulped out loud. "Oh, I'm fine, really. Just a little, um, warm. That tea sounds good." She couldn't change the subject fast enough.

Once the drinks were prepared, Ellie and her mother settled into chairs in the living room.

"You want to tell me about it?" her mother finally said, stirring her tea, but keeping her gaze fixed on Ellie.

It took every bit of willpower she could muster not to squirm under her mother's gaze. Conditioned response, Cheryl had called it—something she'd learned in psychology class. As a child, usually when she was hiding the truth, Ellie had seen that look on her mother's face many times. It had always made her squirm. This time Ellie refused to budge, though her eye rebelled and twitched anyway.

"Ellie?"

"Huh? Oh, uh, well—" She struggled to find the words. Her mother patiently waited. "Do you have any chocolate?"

"Eleanore Rene Williams. Chocolate is not life's answer for every problem," her mother half scolded, already rising for the chocolate.

"No, but it sure helps," Ellie teased.

Walking back into the room with a bag of miniature chocolate bars, she tossed it to Ellie. "Now, spill your guts."

Ellie's head jerked up to her mother who never talked like that. Her mother laughed. "Well, out with it."

"Okay, okay," Ellie said, unwrapping the first chocolate bar. "It's like this, um, I think I'm—well—" she swallowed hard "—I think I'm in love."

"Why, Ellie, that's wonderful, honey."

Ellie was astounded. "Really?" Ellie stared at her a minute. "Why aren't you surprised?"

"I've been expecting it."

"You have?"

Her mother nodded. "Cole Preston, right?"

Ellie frowned. "How did you know?"

"I knew it from the first day you complained about him going to the carpet place to talk to your clients."

Ellie's mouth gaped. "How do you know these things?" She shook her head. "I'll never be a good mom. I don't catch on to things like you do."

Her mother smiled. "You will, when the time comes." Debbie Williams stood and walked over to the sofa to sit down at the opposite end to Ellie. "Now, tell me all about it."

Cole pulled up to the drive-through and ordered a drink. He needed something cold to wake him up, bring him to his senses. He gave his order, dug the money from his pocket, and edged his car to the take-out window. After getting his pop, he stuffed the straw into his cup and drove away. He took a couple of swigs of his drink and decided to drive awhile, heading toward the country roads. He needed to sort through things.

Suddenly, he wanted to push aside his emotions and get practical. The fact that Ellie had mentioned the partnership unnerved him a little. It still weighed on her mind, or she wouldn't have brought it up, teasing or not.

As he drove down one country road, then another, his mind worked through the problems at the office, his feelings for Ellie, everything. By the time he had returned home, he was no closer to settling anything, but one thing was certain. His feelings for Ellie Williams were definitely changing.

The next day, Ellie walked past Cole's office just as he slammed the phone down. She glanced in. "Everything all right?"

With frustration, his hand brushed through the side of his hair. "That man makes me crazy," he said, staring at the top of his desk, as if something important lay there.

"Who?" Ellie slipped into a chair.

"Bob Emerson."

She groaned, knowing full well how the man liked to complain. "What is it this time?"

His head jerked upright. "Oh, this time he has a list. Wants to go over all the problems with the house, at the house, at three o'clock this afternoon. He's bringing his attorney."

"Oh, Cole, I'm sorry. Does Jax know?"

He shook his head. "Emerson just told me on that phone call. Jax won't even be in today, he's at the Persons' job site."

"Anything I can do to help?"

"Yeah. Pray."

* * *

Ellie glanced at the clock. With her house closing scheduled in half an hour, she decided she'd better scoot. She grabbed her files, stuffed them into her briefcase, and headed for the door. "Alex, I'm going to my closing, then off to lunch. After that, I'm going over to one of the job sites. Be back around, say, three-thirty."

"Okay," Alex said sweetly.

Though things were still a little strained with Alex, Ellie felt they were getting better around the office. Alex seemed to have finally accepted Jax's rejection and moved on.

By the time Ellie got back to the office, it was close to four o'clock. As tired as she felt, she probably should have just gone home.

"Hi, Alex," she said, walking past Alex's desk and heading for the kitchen. Alex looked odd, as if something was wrong. Great. Just what Ellie needed, one more thing to deal with today. Things probably hadn't gone well in Cole's meeting with Bob Emerson. Wait, it was just now four o'clock. He wouldn't be finished already.

Ellie grabbed a diet drink from the fridge and headed toward her desk. When she rounded the corner, she saw Cole standing at her desk, a frown on his face. He held a slip of paper in his hand. Worry lined the faces of her coworkers or was it fear? Ellie couldn't imagine what was going on.

"Ellie, will you come to my office, please," Cole asked.

"Sure." She dropped her briefcase, grabbed a pen and paper and her drink, then followed him.

He closed the door and motioned for her to sit down. She did. He held up a telephone message and handed it to her. The message was to him from Bob Emerson, saying simply, "Change appointment. One o'clock. Ellie." It was typewritten on the only electric typewriter in the office that everyone used.

"You want to tell me why I didn't get this?" He was breathing heavily, as if trying to stay calm, though he could blow any moment.

Ellie was confused. Though the message had her name on it, she couldn't remember taking it down. She looked at it once more. It was puzzling, but she'd just tell Cole the truth. "I didn't take the message."

"Just like you didn't order the carpet, right?"

"What?" Had she heard him right? Okay, she could feel anger rising.

"Just what do you mean by that, Cole?" she asked in measured tones, trying to calm the shaking in her voice.

"Well, come on, Ellie, what am I supposed to think? Do you have any clue how mad this guy is? I missed his appointment. He still has to pay his attorney for his time in going there. Of course, he's billing *me* for it. He said you told him it would be no problem for me to get there."

"Let me see that again," Ellie said, practically yanking the paper from him. "Oh, of course there's no time on here. How convenient. I've been gone since before my closing. When did he call?"

"I don't know."

"Why do you automatically assume I'm behind this?"

"Look, I know this isn't like you. Are you feeling okay?"

She stared at him.

"I mean, look at this, Ellie, it does have your name on it."

Well, duh. What was she thinking? "I don't

know what to say. I didn't do it. Period. Why would I type a phone message? When have I *ever* typed a phone message? If you don't believe me, you don't believe me." She stood and started for his door.

"We'll have to talk to Jax about this when he comes back tomorrow."

She whirled around. "Are you threatening me?"

"Come on, Ellie, all I know is strange things are happening around here, and your name is stamped all over them."

She glared at him. "Seems I remember you telling me to trust you once. That's an interesting word. *Trust.* Not easy to do, though, is it, Cole?" She yanked open the door and stomped out, trying hard to keep her tears in check.

# Chapter Eighteen

Cole and Ellie pretty much stayed away from each other over the next few days. Cole couldn't make sense of things. It seemed Ellie was forgetting calls, incoming and outgoing. She was ordering supplies from the wrong places. He even wondered if she could be sick.

One glance at his watch confirmed what his stomach had been telling him. It was lunchtime. No wonder the office was so quiet. He decided he might as well grab a sandwich. He locked the office door behind him and got into his car. Barely making it around the block, Cole remembered he had wanted to drop off some house plans while he was out, but he had left them at the office. He swung the SUV around and pulled back into the parking lot. Oh, good, Alex's car was there. He wouldn't need to get out his office key.

He walked up to the office and pushed on the doors. They were still locked. He hated to disturb her, so he pulled out his office key and unlocked the door. When he pushed through, Alex wasn't at her desk. Probably eating her lunch in the kitchen, he figured. He decided to leave Ellie a note that he would be dropping off the house plans. He walked down the hall and found Alex sitting at Ellie's desk, rummaging through her bottom drawer. Her back was to him.

"Hi," he said.

Alex jumped and whirled around with a start. Her face looked flushed.

"Are you okay?"

"Uh, yes. You startled me, that's all. I—I— was just, um, looking for something. No big deal." She got up from the chair.

Cole nodded. "I was going to leave Ellie a note so I wouldn't have to disturb you, but since I already have disturbed you, I guess I'll tell you."

Alex offered a weak smile, her hand next to her throat. "What do you need?"

"I'm going to drop off some house plans

with the framers so I won't be back till around two o'clock."

"Oh, no problem. I'll let Ellie know."

"Great." He started to turn. "You sure you're all right?"

"Oh, I'm fine," she said with a wave of her hand. She'd already started back toward her desk.

Cole shrugged. "Okay, well, I'll see you later." He disappeared into his office, grabbed the blueprints, and headed outside to his car. Once he had pulled out into traffic, he started thinking. What was Alex doing at Ellie's desk? Whatever it was, she looked like the cat who had swallowed the canary. He thought a moment longer. Maybe she was caught off guard, just nervous because she was in the office alone. Still, why was she rummaging through Ellie's desk?

Something didn't set right with him on this. Maybe he'd better check things out. It's not that he thought she would purposely cause problems in the office. Besides, Jax was the source of her anger, why would she take it out on Ellie?

He wasn't sure exactly what he would do, but he definitely needed to look into the matter. Alex had been after him, trying to get him to go out. Maybe he'd spend a little time with her to see if she would reveal anything. He'd talk to Jax about it and get his take on the matter.

Ellie grabbed a glass in the kitchen cupboard, took some aspirin for her headache and went back to her desk.

"You okay?" Alex asked.

Ellie turned to her. "Oh, yeah, thanks. I'm fine. Just have a headache."

Alex nodded. "Um, Cole wanted me to tell you he'll be back around two o'clock. He had to drop off house plans with the framers."

"Okay, thanks," Ellie said, turning back to her computer screen.

Alex didn't move. "He sure is a nice guy, isn't he?"

Ellie turned to her. "Who?"

"Cole."

"Oh, yeah, he's nice," Ellie said, wondering where this was leading.

Alex inspected her nails. "You know, I never understood why you two never dated. Guess you just weren't his type."

Alex put her hand down and looked at Ellie. Why, Ellie was positively speechless. But even if she had found her voice, Alex didn't give her time to say anything. "Did you ever meet Cole's brother, Caed?"

Ellie wasn't sure how to answer that, since she hadn't met him as Caed. She said simply, "No."

"I've never mentioned this to anyone. Caed told me that Cole was planning to take over the business soon."

"Well, I know Jax would like that."

Alex raised her brows. "I don't think Jax is ready for that just yet. He needs the money to finish school."

"What are you saying, Alex, that Cole wants to force Jax out?"

She shrugged as if to say that's exactly what she meant.

"I don't think Cole would ever do that."

"I'm only telling you what Caed told me."

"Well, I don't know why Caed would say that, but I don't believe it."

Just then, Morgan and Chad walked into the room. "Well, I'd better get back to work," Alex said.

Ellie thought about what Alex had said. It couldn't be true. Cole wasn't a permanent kind of guy. She couldn't see him planning to take the business from Jax. He wouldn't want to be saddled with it. At least, she didn't think he would. But what if Caed did say that? And what if it was true? Maybe Cole was behind the mysterious happenings in the office. That would mean Jax was in trouble.

To make matters worse, Jax trusted him completely.

"Cole, come on in," Jax said, as he opened the door wide for Cole to enter the house.

"Sorry to bother you so late, but I thought I'd better talk to you here rather than at the office."

"No bother. I just finished studying, and I'm ready to relax. You want something to drink?" Jax headed for the kitchen and Cole followed.

"You have any pop?"

"Sure do." He plopped some ice into glasses and poured them each a full glass. "Let's go in the living room," he said, leading the way.

After they had settled into their seats, Jax took another sip of his drink and set his glass on a coaster on the coffee table. "Now, to what do I owe the pleasure?"

"Um, I don't know that I have any basis for this, but I just wanted to share my concerns with you," Cole began. Then he proceeded to tell Jax his feelings about the recent problems in the office and how he wondered if Alex was behind them.

Jax ran his hand through his hair. "Boy, I don't know, Cole. Alex might be spoiled and a little self-centered, but I wouldn't have imagined her capable of stirring up that kind of trouble. Are you sure it's not just a fluke? I mean, the carpet, the missed appointment. Those things happen. Maybe it's nobody's fault really. We all make mistakes."

"Maybe. But I have a feeling it's more than that."

They talked awhile longer and by the time Cole got ready to leave, they had decided to keep an eye on things, but not to do anything rash. Cole let Jax know he was going to spend some time with Alex just to see if he could find out anything, but he didn't want Jax to think there was anything going on between the two of them.

"Look, Cole, it wouldn't matter if you did want to date her. She's free. Alex is a nice woman, she's just not for me."

"Well, she's not right for me, either. I already have my sights on someone."

"Ellie?"

Cole smiled.

"I thought so. I knew it was just a matter of time. If she hadn't seen me like a brother from the get-go, though, you wouldn't have stood a chance."

Cole laughed. "Thanks, bro. I appreciate it."

Jax laughed with him while they walked to the door. He put his hand on Cole's shoulder. "Just be careful. If Alex is doing these things, it's rather serious. Who knows what she might do next?"

"You be careful, too. You're the one she's trying to hurt, you know."

Jax winced. "I guess you're right."

Cole stepped through the door. "I'll be praying for you."

"You, too."

When Ellie walked into work the next morning, there was a definite chill to the air inside the office. Everyone sat at their desks working, which wasn't unusual, but no one looked up when she walked in or uttered a greeting of any kind. The room was eerily quiet.

Once she had settled into her chair, she reached over to start her computer. Cole's voice stopped her.

"Don't bother turning that on."

She swiveled around in her chair and looked at him. "Why not?"

"Come to my office."

She picked up her paper and pen and followed him. He closed the door behind them once they were inside his office.

When he sat down, she got a good look at him. Dark circles framed his eyes, whiskers shadowed his face. "Cole, what's going on?"

He took a drink of what looked like cold coffee and made a face. "Our computer crashed. Lost all the house plans. Everything. We're done. I don't see any possible way of fixing this."

"What about the backups we do each night?"

"Destroyed. Whoever did this saw to it that we were ruined."

"This was deliberate?"

"No question. Jax will have to bring in the authorities."

Ellie thought about what Alex had told her. Could this be an act? Did Cole bring about this disaster to get Jax to fold early so Cole could take over? He hung his head, staring at the desk in front of him. She studied him. She couldn't imagine him capable of such things. Still, doubt nagged at her.

She could have the answer to the computer problem, but wasn't sure she should tell Cole just yet. Not until she knew whom she could trust.

"Well, I just wanted you to know. Work on your phone calls, do what paperwork you can until the computer people come in here and tell us what they can do."

"Okay." She stood. "I'm sorry," she said before exiting the room, leaving Cole in his misery.

Cole wanted to throw up. This was the worst mess he'd ever seen. What bothered him was Ellie didn't seem all that surprised or upset. Didn't she understand the enormity of the problem? Perhaps she didn't care.

He took another drink from his coffee cup. One sip and he pushed it aside. It was cold and horrible. This problem was beyond him. They needed God's intervention. It irritated Cole to no end that he didn't know who was behind this sabotage in the company. He needed to spend some time with Alex, see what he could find out. He refused to believe Ellie could do such things. Surely his heart wasn't in the way of his good judgment, was it?

* * *

Ellie's heart weighed heavy in her chest. A cloud of gloom seemed to hang over the office. She'd better get home and see if she could find the CDs. First, she'd get some coffee, finish up the things on which she had been working, then she'd make an excuse to leave. Maybe even wait until lunch to go so no one would get suspicious. She didn't want to get their hopes up for nothing. After all, she hadn't checked the backup to make sure it was working. She felt stupid about that. It only made sense to do so, but for some reason, she hadn't given it a thought.

She stopped short of the kitchen when she overheard Jax and Cole talking. Not wanting to eavesdrop, she turned to go back to her desk and give them their privacy, but Jax's words stopped her cold.

"I'm telling you, Cole, I want out. I can't take it anymore. I wanted out before the problems, but this just confirms the matter for me. If you don't want the business, I'll sell it to someone else. Someone who has an eye for business and can see the potential."

Alex's words played over in Ellie's mind. Ellie felt sick. She didn't want to believe that Cole had set this whole thing up in an effort to take over the business. Everyone knew Jax eventually wanted out, why would Cole take these measures now? It didn't make sense. He would have been given the opportunity to take it over, so why did he need it now? Alex had tried to imply that Cole had said the place was a gold mine and Jax wouldn't recognize a good business if it hit him over the head. The words hurt her even now. She loved Jax. And Cole. Oh, what could she do?

"You okay, Ellie?" Alex called behind her.

Ellie swallowed hard and nodded. She walked back to her desk, feeling embarrassed that Alex had caught her eavesdropping. She decided the best thing she could do was pray. So she did. She could hardly wait to get home at lunch and check the CDs.

The computer repair guys came in to work on the system. Ellie walked to Cole's office to let him know she was going to lunch. When she reached his door, she couldn't believe what she saw. There stood Alex inches from him, staring up into his eyes, her hand about to caress his face. Ellie found it hard to swallow. Cole looked up.

"Ellie, come in."

She glanced at Alex who didn't seem to

mind in the least being caught in their romantic moment.

"I—I just wanted to let you know I was leaving for lunch," Ellie said, not daring to look at them.

Cole pulled away from Alex and walked toward Ellie. "Okay, Ellie." He reached for her arm, causing her to look at him. "Thanks for your help this morning." His gaze held hers for a moment, then she glanced at Alex who lifted her chin and quirked an eyebrow.

"I'll be back in a little while," Ellie managed, pulling herself free from Cole's touch. She walked from the office, her pulse pounding hard against her ears.

She couldn't get home fast enough. Nothing made sense. Cole and Alex. In this together, out to destroy Jax. Why? Not only was she losing the man she loved, but he was destroying her best friend in the process.

Once in her house, she knelt at her bedside and prayed for the office and all that was going on. She prayed for Jax. Although a bit reluctantly, she prayed for Cole and Alex. Only God could bring them all through this situation.

After prayer, Ellie washed her face and walked into her computer room. There on the desk were the CDs she hoped would save the day. Turning on the computer, she checked first one CD, then the next in the drive. The backup was complete as of last Friday. So, they had only lost what had been put on the computer for the last three days. Great news. Praying Jax would still be at the office, Ellie pulled out the last CD, placed it in the plastic case, and stuck it in her purse.

By the time she arrived back at the office, Jax was just walking into the parking lot. She shut off her engine, grabbed her purse, and climbed out of the car. "Jax, may I talk to you a moment?" she said with a wave of her hand.

He turned and walked wearily toward her. His face, pale and tight, held defeat. "Yeah, Ellie, what do you need?" he asked, the usual light gone from his eyes.

Her pulse quickened, knowing the CDs would improve his spirits. She reached into her purse. "Did you remember that I still do backups at the end of each week? I went home and got the CDs. These are the back-ups to what was on the computer up to last Friday."

It seemed to take a fraction of a second for the meaning to hit him. He looked at her, mouth gaping, then hope lit his eyes. Jax pulled her into a tight embrace, lifted her, then swirled her around a couple of times. "Jax, put me down," she said with a giggle.

Just then Cole and Alex walked into the parking lot. "Well, I'm glad someone is happy," Cole said, appearing a bit put out by their little display.

Jax laughed and put Ellie down. He lifted the packet of CDs from her hand and waved them. "Ellie has saved the day. She's been backing up our hard drive at the end of each week and taking them home. It's something I asked her to start doing, I don't know, about six months ago. I totally forgot about it. We had decided it would be a good thing to have backups somewhere other than the office in case of a fire or whatever. I wanted her to do it because I trusted her, and I didn't trust myself to remember to do it." He laughed and pulled Ellie close to him, placing a firm kiss on her cheek.

Relief washed over Cole, making him look years younger. "Now, it's my turn." He pulled Ellie into an enormous embrace and hugged her tight. When he released her, he looked at her, cupping her chin in the palm of his hand. "Thank you, Ellie."

She shivered beneath his touch.

"Are you ready to go, Cole? They won't hold our reservations forever," Alex said in a way that indicated she wanted Ellie to know they were going to lunch together.

"Oh, sure."

"Congratulations, Ellie," Alex said.

For some reason, Ellie didn't think Alex meant it.

## Chapter Nineteen

The hostess walked Alex and Cole to their table. The room buzzed with activity as people crowded the restaurant for lunch.

Once they had ordered their meals and received their drinks, Cole felt himself relax. "Boy, I can't tell you how much better I feel that Ellie had those CDs. I just wonder why she didn't tell us this morning? Would have saved us a lot of worry."

Alex's eyebrows raised. "Does make you wonder, doesn't it?"

Cole didn't respond. Alex reached over and cupped her hand on Cole's. "I want to thank you for being such a good friend, Cole." She smiled sweetly, making him want to squirm. "I wondered if you'd consider coming to my home for dinner tonight?"

"Well, I don't know—"

Her bottom lip puckered. "Oh, please. I have the best lasagna recipe, and you just have to try it."

Cole thought a moment. Maybe something she would say or do would cast more light on what was going on in the office. He had wanted to spend time with her, after all, try to get to the truth of things. But an actual date, well, he wasn't sure about that.

She rubbed his hand. "Please, say you'll come."

With a touch of discretion, he eased his hand from under hers. "I suppose that would work for me," he said, glancing around the restaurant, trying not to give her the impression he was interested in her romantically.

"Oh, wonderful." She clapped her hands. "How about seven o'clock?"

"Okay. You'll have to give me directions to get there."

"No problem."

They passed lunch in casual conversation, and by the time they arrived back at the office, Cole had no better handle on the sabotage in the office than he had had before lunch.

When they entered the office, they found

Ellie at the front desk, talking on the phone. Alex reached over and squeezed Cole's hand, a gesture he noticed Ellie caught. He felt as if he was trapped in a web and Alex was the spider, toying with him. Not wanting to give Alex the wrong impression, he wasn't at all sure he wanted to go to her house. If he could just get to the truth of things, he could forget all these games. Now that the computer was saved, he wondered if Jax still wanted to leave or if that had been discouragement talking.

Ellie hung up the phone.

"Thank you for lunch, Cole. I had a great time," Alex said loudly enough for Ellie to hear. He glanced at Ellie. Their eyes locked a moment. Then Ellie picked up her notebook and turned toward her desk. He glanced back at Alex. A challenge lit her eyes. She was up to something. He needed to get to the truth.

Over coffee that night, Ellie told Cheryl everything that had been happening at the office. "I'm telling you, Cheryl, they deserve each other."

"I'm not convinced they're in on it together, Ellie."

"Oh, please. Out to lunch, then I heard Alex talking to him about dinner tonight."

"Are you jealous?"

The words pierced Ellie's heart. She didn't answer.

Cheryl squeezed her friend's hand. "Look, El, don't give up on him yet, okay?"

Tears pooled in Ellie's eyes. "I thought we had something between us. I've been so stupid."

Cheryl reached into her purse, pulled out a tissue, and handed it to Ellie. "Oh, no, you haven't. I still think he cares for you. Give it time. See how it all shakes out."

Ellie dabbed at her eyes. "She told me Cole felt really bad about what Caed did to me. Can you believe he told Alex about that?" Her voice rose in pitch. "As if it wasn't humiliating enough without him spreading it around the office."

"I know it looks bad and sounds bad, Ellie, but I don't trust Alex. I'm telling you, get to the bottom of things before you do anything rash."

They each drank from their coffee cups a moment. "I'm going to stay clear of him, mind my own business. I'm trying to stick things out for Jax. But if Jax sells the business to Cole, then I'll know for sure Cole and Alex had arranged it all along. One thing I know, I won't stick around if Cole buys the business."

Cheryl nodded slightly, but kept silent. "Well, whatever you decide, I will be praying for you," she said finally.

"Thanks, Cheryl. I would never make it through this without you."

After dinner, Alex sat down close to Cole on the sofa. Soft music swirled in the room while candles flickered from the fireplace mantel. She turned to him, her fingers smoothing the hair behind his ears. "Thank you for coming tonight," she whispered close to his ear. So close, he could feel her breath on his neck.

He swallowed hard, not liking where this was going.

"You know, I knew the moment I met you there was something special about you, but I was stuck with Jax at the time." She kissed his temple lightly. He didn't want to embarrass her, so he gently tried to ease away from her touch. But she held him firm. "I wasted time with him." Her long nails tickled the other side of his face, then she turned his face to look at her. Before he could get away, in one bold sweep, she leaned her head in and kissed him hard, all the while running her fingers through the back of his hair. He could feel her trying to lure him in like a fly to a web.

Cole jerked away. "I've got to go," he said, trying to stand.

Alex grabbed at him. "Cole, you can't leave. What's wrong? You know you want to stay."

Not wanting to hurt her, but wanting to make it clear he was not interested in her in that way, he took a long, deep breath. "I've got to go, Alex. I don't know what you're trying to do here, but leave me out of it, okay?" At that point, he didn't care if he couldn't get her to confess to the office sabotage or not. Things were getting out of hand.

A pained expression flickered across her face, then she rose to stand within inches of his face. "What's the matter, Cole, don't you trust yourself with me?" She lifted her hands to his chest.

He grabbed her wrists and pushed them down. "I trust myself completely with you, Alex. Actually, it's you I don't trust." He took a step back.

Her eyes narrowed and looked as hard as rocks, her jaw set. She stepped toward him. "You afraid Ellie will find out about us?"

The sound of her voice sent a chill up his spine. "Leave Ellie out of this."

"Poor little Ellie. Everybody worries about poor little Ellie." She practically spat Ellie's name. "I would have thought your brother's little game would have made her wise up."

Cole stared at her in disbelief. He wanted to ask her how she knew, but then, working in a small office, nothing could stay hidden for long. Even office sabotage. Looking at the hard glint in her eyes, the firm line of her mouth, the strong lock of her jaw, Cole suddenly realized he had his answer. Alex had to be the one behind the office sabotage. Though it surprised him, he found himself pitying her.

"I'm sorry, Alex. You're a good friend, but—"

"Friend," she sneered. "I don't want to be your friend."

The expression on her face sickened him. He needed to get out of there and fast. "Look—"

She took a deep breath as if to calm herself. "It's your loss, Cole." With a cold, measured voice she said, "I promise you, you'll live to regret this."

The next morning Alex walked into Cole's office, walked behind his chair and placed a cup of coffee to the side of him on the desk. She brushed the backs of her fingertips against his cheek. Then as if telling a secret, she bent close to his face. "I thought you might like some coffee, Cole."

Before he could respond, he looked up to see Ellie standing in the doorway. Her face flushed. "Oh, I'm sorry," she mumbled, "I didn't know you were busy." She quickly disappeared.

"Ellie, wait!" he shouted after her. He emerged from his office in time to see the women's bathroom door close. Why did women do that, always go to the bathroom when things got tough?

He figured Alex had known Ellie would be coming to his office. She had planned that whole scene for Ellie's benefit, he felt sure. Wanting to give Alex a piece of his mind, he stomped back to his office, but Alex was gone. He blew out a hard breath and closed his door. He didn't want to deal with Alex right now. It was all he could do to get through the day.

\* \* \*

Ellie had never been so uncomfortable at work. She couldn't stay there. Alex and Cole deserved each other. She'd warn Jax of what they were up to and then she'd leave. There had to be other jobs out there. Somehow she'd manage.

Walking down the hall to Jax's office, she was disappointed to see that his light was off. She had thought he would be at work by now. Just as she turned around to leave, she heard whispers coming from his room. This time, she unashamedly stepped closer. She didn't care if she was eavesdropping, weird things were going on around here, and she wanted to get to the bottom of it.

"I'm not paying you until you get the job done, Ed. I told you that already. When the guys finish the job on Tulip Drive, they'll get their money. Don't you ever call me here. Call my cell phone. I'll bring the spray cans and the paint. The place is deserted since it's the first house in the subdivision. You guys meet me there around midnight, and I'll let you in. You'll get paid once the job is done."

Ellie's breath caught in her throat. So that was her plan. Alex was behind all this. She'd let Jax know and the two of them could catch them in the act. One thing for sure, she wouldn't tell Cole.

"What are you doing?" Cole asked.

Ellie swung around. "Oh, I was just getting ready to tell Jax something, but he's not here." She whisked on past a puzzled Cole. As she rounded the corner, she peeked back at him to see him looking in at Alex, then he looked back toward where Ellie had been. She ducked her head.

Those two were definitely up to something.

Ellie went back to her desk and worked awhile. Once she heard Jax come in, she went in to see him.

"Could we talk a minute?"

"Sure, come on in," he said, indicating that she should close the door.

Ellie explained to him what she had heard Alex saying over the phone. Ellie wanted to know if he would come with her that night in hopes of catching the perpetrators in action.

"I'll be glad to go, Ellie, but I've got to tell you, I know Cole isn't behind this." He held up his hand to stop her protest. "I know he isn't behind this." His voice held authority. "Cole and I meet regularly to study the Bible.

I think I know him pretty well. He's on our side."

She held perfectly still.

He sighed. "I can see you're not convinced, so I won't bring him along, but I'm telling you, he's a good guy."

"I suppose that's why he wants to take over the business?"

"He does?" Jax's face brightened. "Did he tell you that?"

Ellie frowned. "How can you say that, Jax? Why are you letting him do that?"

"Letting him do that?" he asked incredulously. "I *want* him to do that. I've been practically begging him to do that for the past couple of months."

"Only because he's setting you up so that you feel you have to get away."

"Look, Ellie, I don't know where you're getting your information, but I talked to Cole about this before he ever came on board. We agreed to a trial-basis thing, but the idea was that if he liked the business and wanted to stay on, he had the first option to purchase it. I do not want to stay here. I've never wanted to own this place, you of all people should know that."

"I thought you needed it for a while to put

you through school." She looked at him for answers, her own piecing together of the puzzle falling apart.

"That's part of the deal. He buys the business, and I get to stay on for a designated length of time at a certain salary, providing the sales merit it. It's all spelled out in the contract. The contract which he has yet to sign. As far as I know, he's still not sure this is what he wants to do."

"Let me get this straight. He's not forcing you out?"

He shook his head.

"You want to go," she said more than asked.

He nodded.

"You believe in Cole Preston, and you feel he's working for the good of the business?"

He nodded again, with a smile.

She felt stupid for believing Alex's lie. Then she thought of something else. "What about Alex? They've been, well, a little tight lately, and if she's up to no good, doesn't that incriminate him?"

"They're not 'tight,' as you call it. She's trying to pull him in. Cole wants no part of it. He's been keeping me informed all along the way."

"I don't know that I'm convinced," she said stubbornly.

"Doesn't matter, Ellie. *I* am convinced." His tone let her know the matter was settled. "I'll be by to pick you up around eleven-thirty tonight, okay?"

"Okay," she said, feeling a little dejected that her theory didn't work out. Still, she couldn't help wanting to believe Jax about Cole's innocence. "See you tonight."

"There's a red truck turning in," Ellie said, pointing.

"Here," Jax said, handing her his cell phone. "Call the police. I'm going over there."

"Wait. I'll go with you."

He waited a moment while she called the police and gave them the details, then together they walked over to the house. The driver had hidden the truck behind a group of trees.

"We need to be careful, Ellie. These guys could be dangerous."

She nodded. A twig snapped beneath Jax's boots, causing Ellie to jump.

Once they arrived at the house, they sneaked up onto the porch and Jax turned the door handle. The door was locked. Ellie pulled out a key. "I was afraid they would make it hard for us to get in, so I brought the spare key," she whispered.

"Good girl," Jax whispered back and gently pushed in the key, letting them in. Quietly, they slipped into the room. A man stood in the corner of the room, as if searching for a place to hide. Ellie looked around, she didn't see anyone else. She was afraid others were lurking in the bedrooms, but before she could say anything, Jax pulled out a flashlight and beamed it on the man.

"Game's over, buddy."

The man whirled around, the light revealing his identity.

Ellie gasped when she looked upon the face of the man. All her hopes vanished in the light on his face. She had wanted to be wrong. But the truth stared back at her in living color. The man who had won her heart stood before them now as nothing more than a common criminal.

The man, her man. Cole Preston.

# Chapter Twenty

Cole's hands were up. "It's not what you think."

"What are you doing here, Cole?" Jax asked with disbelief in his voice.

"Well, I'll tell you," Cole whispered and waved his hand, "if you'll step away from the window and shut off that light."

Jax and Ellie moved out of view, and Jax turned off the flashlight.

"Okay, we're waiting," Ellie said with impatience.

"I'm here doing the same thing you're doing. Trying to get to the truth."

"I don't believe you," Ellie said, her voice thick with pain.

"Look, I don't have time to argue about it.

The real culprits will be here any minute. I followed them here."

"How did you know they were coming?" Ellie asked, arms folded across her chest.

"You weren't the only one eavesdropping on Alex's conversation today," Cole told her. "Stand back or we'll all be in trouble."

Ellie didn't know what to believe. "Why didn't you say something to one of us?"

"The same reason you didn't say anything to me."

Shame washed over Ellie when she realized Cole knew she didn't trust him.

"Remember the trust thing?" Cole asked.

She wanted to say she was sorry, but she still wasn't sure she was convinced. Jax and Ellie stepped closer to Cole who stood near the window's edge.

Before they could discuss it any further, voices sounded outside. "It's probably the police," Jax said.

Cole peeked from the side of the window. "Unless they're equipped with paint cans and dark hoods, I would say it's not the police," Cole whispered. "Come on, let's go out this way." Cole was already moving toward the back door.

Quickly, the three of them slipped through

the door just as the front door pushed open. "Okay, Alex, where do you want us to spray this time?"

"Everywhere. And make sure you get lots of paint on the carpets. You hardly made a dent in their pocketbooks last time. Hold nothing back, guys. Give it to 'em good."

"Boy, you have a real problem with these guys, don't you?" said one man with a growl to his voice.

"Let's just say no one treats me like that and gets away with it."

"Remind me never to break up with *my* old lady," said another with a coarse laugh.

"Just get to work while I watch outside and make sure no one sees us."

"Walker PD," a voice called behind Jax. The three whirled around. "Jax, you okay?" one of the officers said to him.

"Hey, Jim. Yeah, we're fine. But in the meantime, those jerks are ruining our house."

The officer Jax had called Jim nodded and looked toward the other officer. "You go around front, get anyone who comes out that way," he said, pointing. "I'll come in from behind." He looked toward Jax and company. "You all try to stay out of the way so no one gets hurt."

They nodded in unison.

"I'm going around front in case they try to bolt," Cole whispered to Jax. "You stay and cover this side." Cole turned to Ellie and placed his hands on her arms. "You stay out of the way, okay?"

Though he issued his words like a command, Ellie didn't take offense. She felt something in his touch that made her feel good despite the seriousness of the moment. Maybe later she could turn it over in her mind and analyze it. She stayed back a few feet, but followed Cole around to the front of the house.

The officer slipped in the back door, and Ellie heard him shout, "Walker Police Department, put your hands up."

Two individuals bolted from the front door, one of them a man, whom the officer caught. The other person ran straight toward Ellie. Ellie grabbed the perpetrator and they wrestled to the ground. Breathless from the struggle, Ellie pinned the person in place.

The officer in the front yard handcuffed the man he had caught, Mirandized him, and placed him in the car. In the meantime, Cole and Jax came over to help Ellie. Jax pulled the criminal up from the ground and yanked off the dark hood covering the perpetrator's head and face. Long hair spilled from the cap.

"Alex, why?" Jax asked, pain in his voice.

She merely lifted a smirk toward him.

Officer Jim walked over to them. He handcuffed Alex and recited the Miranda warning. After a few minutes, the police had corralled the lot of them and hauled them into the car. Officer Jim walked back to Jax. "I know it's late, but you'll need to come to the station and give a statement."

They nodded.

The police drove away. Jax, Cole and Ellie stood for a moment in silence, watching as the car left the site.

"I'm sorry, Jax," Ellie offered, knowing her friend had to be hurting just now.

"Yeah, me, too," he said.

They stood a moment longer in the shadows then Cole said, "Let's go check out the damage."

Together they walked into the house and looked into every room to see the extent of repairs needed. Fortunately, the vandals hadn't been in the house long enough to do any real damage. They had only gotten as far as a little paint on the living-room wall. Repairs would be minimal.

By the time Jax, Cole and Ellie left the station, it was two o'clock in the morning. They were too keyed up to go to sleep, so they went to an all-night café for some coffee.

Cole slid into the booth beside Ellie. Jax sat across from them. Once they were settled and their coffees were ordered, Cole turned to Ellie, resting his arm lazily on the booth behind her. "So, you thought I was in on all this?"

She reluctantly lifted her gaze to him, her left eye twitching. He pointed at it and laughed. Her lips pulled into a thin line, and she covered her eye with her hand. "Okay, so I'm not a good detective."

Cole and Jax laughed, then turned to take a drink of the coffee the waitress had placed before them.

"Well, you have to admit things looked a little suspicious," Ellie said.

Cole shrugged. "I could say the same thing about you, you know."

"Me? How?"

"Well, let's just say you've been a little less than friendly from day one. The partnership and all."

She made a face. "Like I care about that

now. Besides, that was Jax's mistake. He had his chance and blew it."

Both men let out a unified "Whoa."

"What do you mean, I had my chance? Are you trying to tell me something here?" Jax asked.

Ellie grew serious. "Well, truthfully, I had considered leaving, and I went so far as to put my résumé out there. But now that things are settled, maybe we can get back to normal."

"Um, well, I'm not sure this is the right time, but I think I need to let you both know something."

Ellie and Jax looked at Cole.

"The ad agency in Chicago where I used to work, well, um, you remember I told you they'd been bought out by new owners?"

Jax nodded. Ellie squirmed in her seat.

"It seems they want me back."

By the following week, things had settled down at work, though Ellie found it hard to concentrate on anything. Needing time to think, she felt glad it was Saturday morning.

She stared aimlessly at her television, a pillow balled up at her stomach. What was the use? She didn't know what was going on with the program anyway. Picking up the remote, she clicked the screen off.

The only man she had ever loved was considering a move. A move far from her. She had come a long way, learned to bend with life's changes, and now this. This was one change she wasn't sure she could ever get over.

This was one problem she couldn't handle alone.

She needed to pray.

Cole signed his name on the purchase agreement and handed the document back to Jax. "You're sure this is what you want, Cole?"

"I'm sure," he said with a smile. "We've been talking about this for months. I've seen the financials, talked with the bank officials. It's all in order."

"And you're okay about the job in Chicago?"

Cole nodded.

Jax studied him. "I think I know what made up your mind for you."

Cole raised his eyebrows.

"Or maybe I should say who."

Cole smiled.

"Ellie Williams."

Cole straightened the paperwork in front of him. "You always did know me well, Jax."

Jax grinned. "So, when are you going to pop the question?"

"I thought you'd never ask." Cole reached into his pocket and pulled out a black ring box. He snapped open the lid and revealed a large solitary diamond on a gold band.

Jax's eyes widened, and he let out a whistle. "Whoa, you are *serious*."

Cole nodded. "I'm going home, get cleaned up, make a couple of stops and head over to her house. I hope she'll be home." Cole thought a moment. "I'm prepared to grovel if it will help."

Jax laughed out loud. "Knowing Ellie the way I do, I don't think she'll make you resort to that."

"You do know her pretty well, don't you?"

Jax nodded.

"Do you think I have a chance?"

Jax rubbed his chin thoughtfully, as if he had to think about it. Cole felt sure Jax was waiting for him to squirm. Cole complied, bringing a smile to Jax's face. "No doubt in my mind that she's loved you for a long time." He paused. "She just didn't know it."

"Well, I hope she knows it now," Cole said, a little apprehensively.

"Oh, I think she knows."

"And do I have big brother's blessings?"

"You've got it, buddy." Jax slugged Cole on the shoulder. "Speaking of brothers, I think you owe this whole thing to Caed."

Cole frowned. "Oh, man, I hate it when he's right. He'll never let me hear the end of it."

Jax laughed again as the two of them left the office. "Let me know when I need to get my tux," Jax shouted across the parking lot.

"Let's just hope you need one," Cole bantered back, before climbing into his SUV.

After settling the matter of Cole with God in prayer, Ellie got up from the sofa and decided to take a shower and get dressed for the day. She took her orange juice glass into the kitchen, rinsed it and glanced out the window.

Despite the fact she hadn't planted her maple tree in the spring, the best time for planting, it looked good. She should probably have waited until the next spring, but for some reason, it was important to her to get it in the ground this year. She shook her head. Seemed silly now, but not when she had planted it. Still, the tree looked healthy, and for that she was grateful. Strong roots, she thought.

Once again her thoughts went to Cole. He'd thought the tree-planting was a dumb idea, she could tell. Probably the talk of roots and commitment didn't set well with him, just as changes had always bothered her in the past. She sighed and turned away from the window.

He would go to Chicago. It just wasn't in his blood to settle down. She walked absently into the living room and straightened the pillows on her sofa. Some men were just like that, she reasoned. Nobody's fault, really. She should have known better than to let her heart get tangled with him. After putting a couple of things in the room back into place, she told herself to stop daydreaming. "Whatever will be, will be," she said with a hint of defeat. She might as well get used to the idea. Nothing she could do or say would change things. Cole would leave for Chicago, and her life would continue as it had always been.

Funny, she'd never thought she'd be the one to want change.

She glanced around the room. With her house already cleaned, she didn't have a lot she had to do today. Shopping always seemed to help her get her mind off her problems. Maybe she'd head over to the department store and check out the fall clothes on display. Might even stop for a mocha at the coffee shop. Mochas always made her feel better. Her thoughts flitted to the chocolate stash in her bedroom drawer. Even that didn't perk her spirits. Alarm rushed through her. This was more serious than she had thought. She'd better go shopping—and fast.

She trudged into her bedroom and pulled out the clothes she wanted to wear: jeans, sweatshirt, athletic shoes. After shopping, she might go over to the park for a while, read her book.

Despite the heaviness in her heart, she felt better after her shower. She didn't know what the future would hold, but she knew who held the future. And God was Someone she could trust.

After Ellie took her shower, finished reading her devotions, talked to her mother and Cheryl on the phone, the day was half spent. She decided she still had time to get to the store and check out some clothes, so she ran a brush through her hair and went to the living room to grab her purse. Just as she reached for it, the doorbell rang.

Leaving her purse by the chair, she walked over and opened the door. To her surprise, there stood Cole at the door, holding a potted tree. He peeked through the branches. "Okay if I come in?"

"Um, sure," she said, pointing for him to put the tree on the hardwood floor at the entryway.

"I thought I would get your opinion on this since you're so good with trees."

Her mind was whirling, what was this about? She couldn't help but let out a guarded smile.

He stood up and brushed his hands together. "The man at the greenhouse said this gets huge over the course of, say, thirty, forty, years."

Ellie stared at him, practically gaping.

"But you're renting your place. Will your landlord let you plant the tree?"

"I'm not staying there. I'm moving."

"Oh," Ellie said, nausea squeezing her stomach. "Why didn't you just wait and buy a tree in Chicago?" She looked back at the tree.

"That seems a long way to go to buy a tree

and bring it back here." His eyes glinted with mischief.

Ellie's head jerked up. "You mean—"

He grinned like a Cheshire cat. "That's right, I'm staying here. I just signed the agreement to purchase Wiley's Dream Homes this morning."

She wanted to throw her arms around him and hold him tight. Her heart raced like an accelerator stuck on high speed with the gear in Park. "That's great, Cole," she said as calmly as her shaking voice would allow.

"Just great?"

She looked at him, trying to understand what he was getting at. "So where are you moving to?"

"I thought I'd leave that up to you."

"To me?" Now she really was confused.

He picked up the potted tree. "You know, when you planted your maple tree, I thought that was the craziest thing I'd ever seen. You talked about roots, commitments, everything I'd run from all my life. But things have changed for me. With God. With you." He looked at the tree and held it out to her. "This is a symbol of that change, and I want to plant it in the yard of our first home—that is, if you'll have me."

She opened her mouth to say something, but couldn't seem to find the air. She felt like a fish thrown up on the sand, gasping for breath. Had she heard him right? Did he say he wanted to plant the tree in the yard of *their* first home—as in her home and his home?

Together?

The same one?

"I believe there's something on that front leaf for you."

She glanced down, tears already making wet tracks down her cheeks. There on the branch sparkled the most beautiful diamond upon which she had ever laid her eyes.

Cole pulled it from the branch and put the tree down. He turned to her. "I'm sorry to do it like this, Ellie. I mean, I would rather take you to some fine restaurant, offer you an evening of candlelight and romantic music, but to be honest, I couldn't wait." He took her hand in his. "Ellie Williams, for the first time in my life, I'm not afraid of commitment. You have taught me what trusting is all about. I will love you till the day I die, and I want to commit my life to you, tangle our roots together deep in the foundation of God's love. Raise a family with you." He paused and took a deep breath. "Ellie Williams, will you marry me?"

She nodded meekly, her face wet with tears. Cole slipped the ring on her finger and pulled her to him, kissing her hair, her eyes, her face, and finally allowing her tears to mingle with the sweetness of their kiss.

When they pulled apart and her tears had subsided, Ellie looked up at him. "I love you, Cole. I have loved you from the first day you turned my world upside down with your policy changes." She laughed and grabbed his hand. "Thank you for helping me see my needs but most of all, for giving me a change of heart."

He pulled her into a warm embrace once again. The strains of "Kumbayah" fringed the edges of her mind, then grew stronger as she snuggled into Cole as if he were a warm blanket. She decided she liked that song after all. The question of whether she had marshmallows popped into her mind, but she pushed it aside.

For now, the tune of the familiar song and the feel of Cole's strong arms around her was enough.

\* \* \* \* \*

Dear Reader,

Ellie Williams struggled with change, and Cole Preston dug his heels in at the thought of commitment, but both learned to deal with life's changes in a positive way.

Some changes we welcome, some we wish would never find us. However, we have a God who remains constant in our ever-changing world. Malachi 3:6 tells us, "I the Lord do not change." His love and mercy never fails. He remains faithful. I know this is true because I asked Him to change my life in 1974 and He has been, and continues to be, my stronghold.

So take heart. If you have experienced turmoil in your life through marriage, divorce, children, grandchildren, career moves, illness or even the death of a loved one, God is there for you and stands ready to meet your needs.

Whether you greet change with open arms, or you run from it, go to God and ask Him to change your life, if you haven't already. This is one change you'll be glad you made. After all, He sent His Son that we might receive a change of heart....

*Diann Hunt*